T0146391

INSINMIND

AFTERNOON SOLIPSISM

Allen Knox

BALBOA.
PRESS

A DIVISION OF HAY HOUSE

Balboa Press books may be ordered through booksellers or by contacting:

Balboa Press
A Division of Hay House
1663 Liberty Drive
Bloomington, IN 47403
www.balboapress.com
1 (877) 407-4847

ISBN: 978-1-9822-2629-9 (sc)
ISBN: 978-1-9822-2633-6 (e)

Print information available on the last page.

Balboa Press rev. date: 05/15/2019

CONTENTS

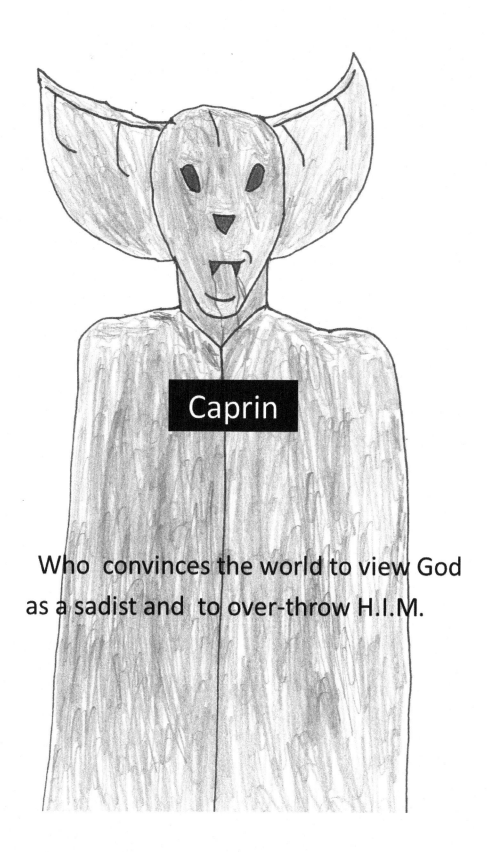

Caprin

Who convinces the world to view God
as a sadist and to over-throw H.I.M.

CHAPTER 1

Formation Of A Tyrant

A SAVIOR? WHO IS a savior? Why wait? And why the suffering?

Is life really about the adoration of being a sadist? Or is there more to it than what we have or what we are taught. Is it what we have as a difficulty to stand? A light so peaceful, a flame glorious! Everything in each other. It was all good before the coming of the stealer. In a snowy, cold land, where the he/she attacks. Nightmares, sin, wickedness and the endurance of limits, are those things that the innocent must face. Hope, faith, love and joy are the boost of the four, that have been covered up with thorns, that are oh so painful to teach.

A bright spark from the Almighty Flame cries out… "I'm fading! I'm fading!" Suddenly the other sparks, which seemed astray said unto the other spark… "Don't do drugs!! Don't do drugs!!" The now fading spark says, "It came to me without a say!" Suddenly many of them faded away from the Almighty Flame forever. Oh! how cold, the snow and ice were upon the land, how forced this spark has become. The land of the he/she seemed to have no sense of mercy pulling it into its mouth of destruction. First licking it, then biting and chewing and finally swallowing it all up. Right before this happens a spark that was a little brighter pushed one of the fading sparks away from the mouth, sacrificing itself to save the less bright spark. Suddenly, now of hopelessness, the fading spark flew towards the Almighty Flame, feeling completely safe in it. The little spark felt, something inside itself. like as if, it was not meant to stay in there yet. And so, the little spark, kept gathering all the other fading sparks within itself, while heading towards the big spark into the almighty flame. But the he/she goat figure knew this, stealing and creating false flames out of fading sparks, that will eventually go into the he/she's mouth, bringing some fading sparks into him/her. The little spark kept trying to get the deceived fading sparks into the almighty flame. Many of the fading sparks did not enter and dissolved into nothing. 'Nothing, the entire nothing…The uncreated, the no god no self-theory'. Eating many ascending sparks into nothing, collapsing because of the one thing that made itself…a no self Aeon. A son that is a son, is not able to open the door to the Almighty Flame. Their light cannot compute with it, and for that order, of the sparks has been misplaced. Only one spark is big enough, to take all the little sparks to the Almighty Flame. The son himself, can never be the son, and the father can never be the father. Oh! How young a little spark is. Oh! How abusive the male/female goat figure is? Oh! How the almighty flame isn't so forgotten unto the little spark. The little spark that is a son but not the son is urged to defend Aeon. Before we get to that spark, let us go into the depths of the goat that wields. One, power for others. Two, Continue or discontinue the beginning of nothing, or the un-bearing. Three, the influence of the pleasures, of the ambition of sin. Four, Them, us and why? A cycle that turns and spins around and around. And Five, Heavy Burden. These are the things that the master tempter of sin, the dark lord Eogo Ali Tainter, has created in a strong usage of wicked energy into our pink maze, that is within our skull. But, why would this goat do such horrible things? What is his/her motive behind this? Is this to over throw the almighty?

A bad childhood? A delusion, or something this soulless creature couldn't bear. Whatever it is that drove this person into that state of mind that it's now in? Is it driven by its own desire? To destroy everything in its path that the Almighty is?

"I'll slaughter you! You hear me? I'll take your horns and stab you through your triangular eye!" Said the four-year-old, covered in acid muck on his body. Eogo just stared at the child for a little bit, he stared almost a whole minute.

"You ruined my entire existence! I'll kill you!! You @#$#%&^*!!!"

Before child could finish his sentence, Eogo, put spiders in his mouth and over his lips, to stop him from speaking. Meanwhile, Eogo, walked down stairs with a book tucked under his left arm, and a golden sword in his right hand. Eogo entered a room with a population numbering eighteen million two hundred and fifty-four thousand, and nineteen people.

Anthropormorthic of all kinds. Monkeys, dogs, cats, tigers all the species in one big giant cocoon. Every one of them moaned in agony due to the roots of the cocoon, squeezing their bodies and tearing their flesh with the thorns engulfed in the roots.

There suddenly appeared a bearded cat-hat around five feet ten inches tall, his name is Jericho Drastic. Jericho Drastic turns and approaches Eogo Ali Tainter looks at him and says, "I have for filled what I have thought to have forbid to for fill. May I please have the duration, speed, and strength of eighteen million?"

Eogo, walked towards the inside of a large green mouth that formed from the cocoon. Inside the mouth a three-foot heart. Two seven-foot Anthropomorthic Grey Hawks with flaming eyes, threw four ox's unto the heart, where they merged with it. Eogo shot a red demon, and it flew towards one of the Anthropomorphic Hawks which are called the Bird Babies. The Bird Baby jumped into the heart merging with it. Eogo looked at the heart like as if he was in such amazement of a painting. For a short moment he looked at Jericho and walked towards the heart and open pages of his book. With his left hand raised into the air forming eighteen million two hundred and sixty-four thousand and nineteen bodies into one organism into the palm of his hand. The Goat blasted the organism at Jericho Drastic, and tossed the Cat Rat into the heart, causing him to merge with it. Dark purple red flaming energy, shot out of Eogo's hands going into the heart, creating a giant red monster. With words calling out "Blood".

Meanwhile with the child,

What is a savior to someone who has great experience and sorrow?
What's the point in doing anything, when the deed is already done?
Why insist in continuing here, if evil is already conquered? Does it even make any sense? Whatever it could be, if you don't follow everything that is good, being something, you turn into evil … of which is nothing.

"Zeth "!!!! Said the male voice, while climbing up the stairs. Then the person with the voice arrived. He was another Cat Rat, with dark long hair, red eyes, pure white skin, black nose, and a mouse tail. His name is Nortric Drastic. "Zeth, don't worry. We are going to get out of this sadistic place, just stay with me ok?"

Year nineteen eighty, June 28th,

Later, on in the news, with a female weasel named Alice Permont, and a male deer named Zack Roundleft. "Last night, the terrorist named Zeth Drastic, has murdered the great Priest hawk Rodsord Septob, and is currently being hunted by Elargarous Yiedon, king of the false world," said Alice "What is next for the news, is, "children finally accepting sadism, upon their flesh. But before we get into that, me and Alice are about to do, a super porn, for your lusting, endless, no hearts content soul." Said Zack.

Meanwhile, in land Insintation,

World of madness, depravity, and wickedness, the land of Insintation is one of the most corrupted places, in the entire Omniverse, that the Almighty is almost to the very edge of annihilating it., but throughout the years of endless sin, he hasn't destroyed it. But why? What's not fully convincing him to do it? Are there still some righteous people there? What could it be?

6:45 PM

Geodesic glass buildings

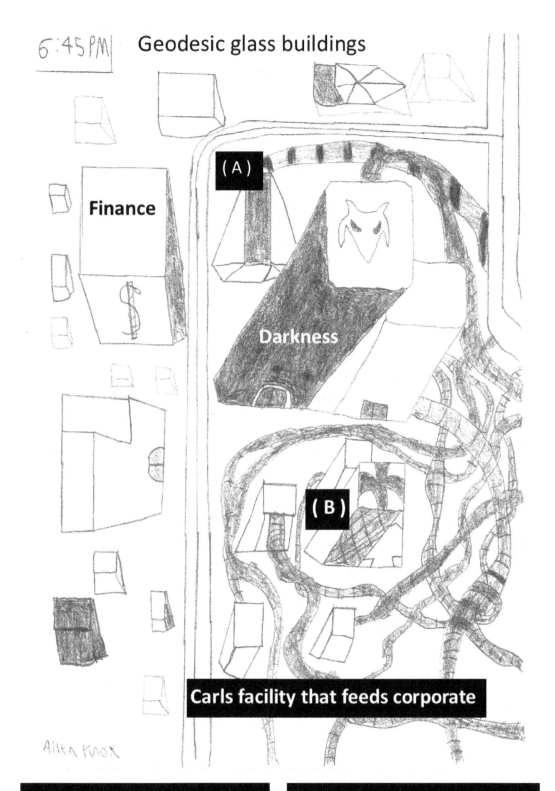

Finance

(A)

Darkness

(B)

Carls facility that feeds corporate

Allen Knox

(A) pump to bird babies   (B) Hospital in city

"Kill the Bully, kill him," said a shadowy figure, channeling energy, on an EIGHT-YEAR-OLD elephant, grabbing the shirt of an EIGHT-YEAR-OLD male serpent bully. For some reason the kids could not see the shadowy figure using dark energy on the elephant.

"I am going to kill you!" Said the elephant child.

The shadowy figure used more energy on the elephant.

"After three and a half years of you hurting me, calling me names, and doing the worst to my mother, freaks like you should have your soul eradicated from existence." "I have waited too long for this. Too long!" Said the elephant child.

Nearly out of nowhere, glowing white energy flows and says," Don't do it! The energy channeled onto the elephant, with the elephant saying, "I want to do this. I want to kill you! But."

The shadowy figure hissed at the white figure. Eventually the appearance of both the shadowy figure, and the bright white figure, began to show. The serpent with glowing purple eyes and brown skin, is named Pansorn Toverd. The bright white figures appearance was a five-foot eleven Cat Rat, with a black hat, black nose, white shirt, dark pants, cat ears, whiskers, red eyes yellow jacket, and a mouse tail. His name is Zeth Drastic. And he is ready to kick some ass. "How dare you interrupt the death of my son? For that your death will be as slow as a decade," but first, Pansorn shot out more energy, onto the elephant, by the words of "Kill him, before it's too late. It is now or never, you moron!"

Zeth, shot out his energy, on the elephant, by using the words, "Think of what your parents would see you as, a child completely torn from the sins of the world? Is that what you want child?" "Do you want to become a soldier of perversion? Because once you put seed in soil, more of the poisonous tree, will grow. Do you really want those trees, to grow? Or do you want to avoid those seeds at all costs?" Said Zeth. The elephant child slowly let go of the serpent child and walked away.

"The Insintation will hear of this! You party pooper, you hear me!" Said Pansorn.

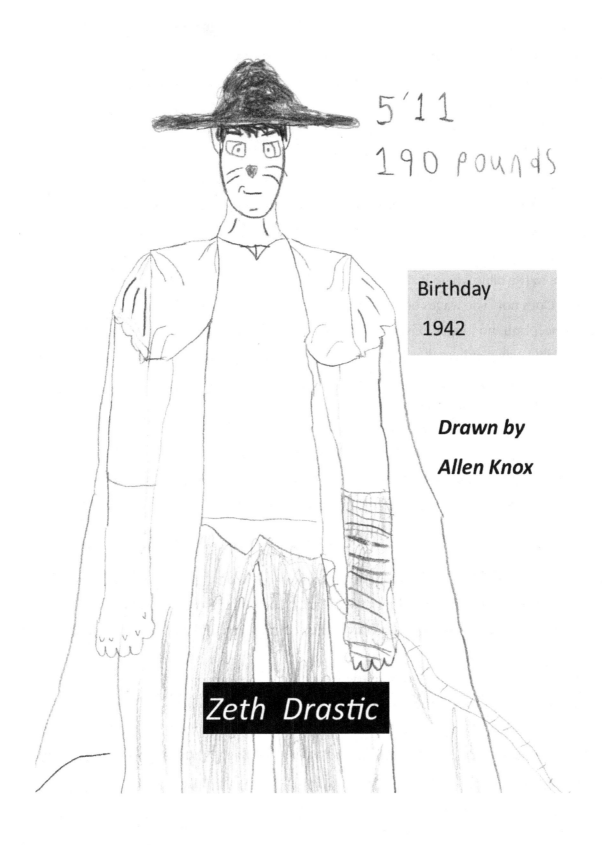

5'11
190 pounds

Birthday
1942

Drawn by

Allen Knox

Zeth Drastic

"I hear you, bro, but the question is, are you going to still be alive and able to do that?" Said Zeth.

"What the hell are you talking about? All I have to do, is tell them. That's all! It's not like you're in my house, killing all of my guards, right?" Said Pansorn.

Zeth smiled, and quickly vanished into thin air. "Oh, don't tell me, please, oh goodness me, no!" Said Pansorn.

Inside Pansorns house, all of his guards, were chopped up into limbs and pieces, by Zeth Drastic. Both Zeth and Pansorn were back into their physical bodies. "How dare you! For this, your torment will be in burning Sulphur forever!" Said Pansorn.

"How is that ever so possible? I mean, wouldn't my body only last, for like gee, I don't know, five seconds maybe? You know I sometimes wonder, if the eternal hell is even real? Because, how in the world, can a sinful body, even last that long? Also, I don't remember, anywhere in the bible where it says that the wicked will have a body meant for in terms of forever." Does not 'The wages of sin is death' mean discontinue? Its like being in the state of preconception, no longer existing. "You get the gig, that's my point here." How is that even possible, when evil, makes it impossible? For the nothing is impossible. I thought all possible, was meant for the faithful? And the impossible, is meant for the unfaithful. So how in the literal hell, are the unfaithful, not to mention sickening, even having eternal life, if they are denying, the only one who can offer it to them. Doesn't life mean exist? And death mean non-existing? Do you even know the difference, between those two? Man, I hate it! When believers use damage control, to support their claim. Call me a shill, all you like, buddy! But damage control in Christians, really upsets the F%^%$#^* out of me." Said Zeth.

"I am not a Christian. I am against that, I am an Insintation, which is anti-Christian. You love the almighty, I hate the almighty. It is as simple as daylight. Do you want to learn the A,B,C, to have an understanding of simplicity. You goof." Said Pansorn.

"I am very sorry for getting carried away there. Now let us fight, before I get bored with the dialogue here." Said Zeth.

The entire floor of the house split in two. Both Zeth and Pansorn, nearly fell twenty-five feet down. Though none of them seem to be hurt by it. "I hope you're really prepared for this?" Said Pansorn. In a green rusty dungeon, a giant eighteen foot, anthropormorphic pig with orange brown leather clothing, and a four-foot dagger. Its name is Belnuff..And its hungry for some Cat Rats.

"RrrOOOOOOAAAAArrrrrrrr!" Said Belnuff.

"Cut his testicals off, Belnuff. And burn his manhood to a crisp!" Said Pansorn.

"Woah nelly, I don't want that knife between my legs." Said Zeth.

Belnuff tried to chop Zeth, but Zeth dodged the attack well, and kicked the giant pig's leg so hard, that the pig fell down hard. Zeth decapitated the head of the giant pig Belnuff and began to walk towards Pansorn.

"I am so screwed, aren't I?" Said Pansorn. Zeth then Karate chops Pansorn, into a hundred pieces.

"What's going on here?" Said the eight-year-old snake.

"I killed a father that didn't give two thoughts about you mister." Said Zeth. "And for that, you are my freaking war hero. I would have saluted you, if I had, had hands." Said the eight-year-old snake.

"Then use your tail." Said Zeth.

The eight-year-old snake, saluted Zeth with his tail, turned and slithered away.

As Zeth got up out of the house, from the top, there was something to him, that didn't feel right. Another shadowy figure, that felt stronger. Much stronger than the previous. Throughout the many sky scrapers, that were over, five thousand feet tall, something, or someone, was watching Zeth. The shaking of fear began to grip with a strong hold on Zeth Drastic. He held onto his four-foot, nine-inch sword, red eyes open wide.

"Oh, heck no! No not this! I can't handle these fights. I just can't handle it. Oh goodness me. He can't be here! How did he find me, Ive got to get out of this place? Oh, Satan damn it! Damn it!" Said Zeth to himself.

As Zeth ran, as fast as he could, to get away from the evil energy, the stronger shadowy figure, was right in front of him, on the top of a thousand-foot building. It was an anthropormorphic seven-foot nine-inch bat, who wielded a six-foot one-inch sword. The bat rises up and says.....

"Good night sadist lover."

Caprin

Zeth eventually had to get a grip on the situation, and charged at the bat. However, the bat charged quicker, creating a huge impact on Zeth's offensive. This sent Zeth flying into another building, crashing through the glass windows. "I can't win, screw this. I can't beat him. I can't do it. I just can't do it." Said Zeth to himself.

Zeth could hear wings flapping, indicating that the bat was near. Zeth jumps up, and runs away, from the sounds of those wings. The sounds stopped, and Zeth was sweating. Suddenly, the bat begins to punch Zeth, on the face nine times, in less than half a second.

The bat clawed his chest, tearing a lot of his skin off, and leaving a few scratches on the bones. Zeth tried to slash the bat with the sword, but the bat blocked five of his attacks, in one fifteenth of a second. In less than zero-point five percent of a second, the bat karate chopped Zeth's neck so hard, that it caused him to bleed.

The karate chop was fueled with dark energy, that triggered and amplifies strong memories of Zeth's past. Zeth began yelling out in a panic. "No, I don't hate him! I can handle the torment! Can you hear me? It is something of my withstanding." Said Zeth. "You think you're a non-sadist lover, but deep down in your mind, you don't seem to be." Said many voices in Zeth's mind.

"I am fully tolerant of it, it's the only way to prove my strength to him. I accept my trial, it is what we all must endure. Evil cannot be destroyed by erasing it. That's what evil is, incarnate, since the beginning, if you could even, call that a beginning that is." Said Zeth.

Both swords were clashing against each other, with their own force and energy. "Evil mixed with good, is like a fading energy, thinking it can outshine darkness, when only the one that existed as long as darkness, can be that energies brethren in doing so." Said Zeth. The bat destroyed Zeth sword easily, and smacked the Cat Rats forehead, with dark energy.

Alone in the black, Zeth hears a familiar voice, that he had not heard in a long time.

"Pre-conception is a belonging for all, it is not necessary to perpetuate, in where rebellion reigns. You know this to be true. You know he is the true rebel. You know it. He lied about reality. He's not a hero Zeth, he's only a savior to the wicked, but he will never be our father. Not before, not now, not ever." Said the distorted voice. "This will never be believable, it is my refusal to deny this checker board mind set. I will break free from this. Now!" Said Zeth. In an explosion of white energy. Zeth ran very fast toward the bat, and did over fifty hand punches, in seventy percent of a second. The bat blocked all of them perfectly, with only his left hand, and did an undercut, on Zeth's jaw. He used one hand only. Zeth crashed up to another level room, and almost didn't get up in time, to defend himself against the bat.

The bat could lift over ten thousand pounds, with a punching speed of, zero point zero zero, forty fifths of a second. The blow to Zeth's arms, felt like an iron pipe, stabbing a child. Even though Zeth was being over powered, he wasn't entirely helpless either. The Cat Rat, can lift over one thousand pounds, has a punching speed of, zero point zero, twenty one percent of a second, and has one of the greatest defenses in combat history, he can defend speeds faster than his offensive speed. However, this is where his defense skills, are put to the ultimate tests and limits.

Zeth begins bleeding from his wrist, his jacket being torn to shreds. The bat knee kicked Zeth on the gas pocket, causing him to gasp and gag for air. By just his left arm alone the bat did eight elbow slams a second, on Zeth's shoulders, causing blood to burst out everywhere from the shoulders. In a fit of rage, Zeth jumped back over 40 feet, and leaped back towards the bat as fast as an arrow. The collision of Zeth's feet, on the bats left hand, caused a shockwave throughout the building. Tearing the building to pieces. The bat prevailed, with relative ease, and karate kicked Zeth on the chest, sending him flying into another abandoned room in just one second. In five seconds, the bat was in the room, and pumbled Zeth like a thug, with only his left fist. Zeth attempted to knee kick the bats belly, but bat defended himself well, with only his left knee blocking it.

The bat jumped up six feet into the air, and kicked Zeth on the nose, sending him flying through three more rooms in less than a second.

"I'm going to lose, the Rightiousful, is doomed to die with me. The Insintation might just be more superior. Are we truly destined to be pre-conceived?" Said Zeth to himself.

Zeth held his hand, flat out and high, with yellow sonic waves coming out. "This is my second to last plan I have to get out of this. I must destroy the Insintation, and the Ali Tainter. I am not ready to defeat his second only, and if I'm not ready to defeat his second only, then I'm definitely not ready to defeat the master, Insintation.. Eogo Ali Tainter." Said zeth.

As the bat delivered his two thousand punches in ten seconds, Zeth blocked them all, by using an ability called 'cordblock'. A power that can offer, near limitless coordination of any attack. In those ten seconds, and afterwards, Zeth felt a horrible feeling on his hands. It was to the point where he couldn't feel a thing. For that his hands were going far beyond the torment.

After the punches were done, the skin of Zeth's right palm, was almost completely peeled away, showing bone. As for his black stitched right arm, it was badly torn, with gushes of blood squirting out of it. Zeth yelled out, loudly, with tears coming out of his eyes, due to the excruciating pain of the bat's punches. The bat grabbed the Cat Rats neck, raising Zeth up, punching him harder and slower. Zeth, coughed blood, while his nose bled, the bat kept beating him up, choking him by the neck. Still holding Zeth's neck, the bat slammed him through the wall. There was over a thousand feet drop, underneath the feet of the Cat Rat. For fifteen seconds the bat looked at Zeth and said. "good luck! enduring this, Drastic traitor." The bat let go causing Zeth to fall over a thousand feet down to the ground level.

Meanwhile, with a female Cat Rat, deep underground, is a disco party, embracing all kinds of sexual sin. With an array of madness showing in the eyes of the Anthropormorphic dancers. Everyone was lusting on flesh, until shreds of energy burst out of them. Which resulted in the end of the party quickly?

Lincent Kaihi Moore

Height / weight 5'0, 85 to 100 pounds	Power comparison Zeth praise [without sinners]	Birthday 1942, August 29th

Her motives are to end sin.

Drawn by
Allen Knox

There was only one person left in that room…. A female Cat Rat, with spikey black long hair, that had two pony tails. She had purple skin, with blue eyes, only, five feet tall. Her bust size engulfed the thirty-eight inches. Her waist was twenty-nine inches around, her hips contoured at thirty-five inches, weighing in at ninety-eight pounds.

Who is this woman? And why is she affiliated with these events? In one word from the female Cat Rat, she says, "zeth."

She ran as fast as a squirrel, getting out of the party. Meanwhile with Zeth. "For out of a thousand years, well sort of, I still can't accomplish jack shit with my goals. Just nothing. I can't forget the life I had to live, in order to be where I am now. The only problem is, my progression is lackluster at best. Besides, I'm even considered, by many people, to fail. So why in the hell, am I doing this anyway.?" Said Zeth to himself.

Barely making out alive from the fall, he only landed on the top part of his back, breaking the spine a little. However, whatever he landed on was just a vehicle. He then remembered what Nortric told him.

Nortric had told him," you can be surprised at what you can do, against enemies as strong or stronger than yourself. I've even seen people conquer enemies, that were almost triple their strength. They beat them with just, their bare fist. Even if you fail Zeth, you might be a little impressed, over what you can do with the more powerful enemies. If an enemy does not have too much over bearing power over you, then darn it Zeth! Get your ass in shape and beat that powerful enemy! In a trot, Zeth raised up, and the bat appeared in front of him. Zeth ran towards the seven-foot nine-inch anthropormorphic bat, and attempted to kick it on the shoulders, however the bat blocked all eight of his attempts in one second. The bat grabbed Zeth's legs, throwing him up, a hundred and twenty feet up in the air. The bat shot out electric plant like energy, right at Zeth, in the air. The Cat Rat ascended to two thousand, five hundred feet, in 5 seconds. Eight Thousand feet in nine seconds, twenty thousand feet in four seconds, and a hundred and eighty thousand feet in twelve seconds. By reaching these altitudes, Zeth barely made it into crash landing on, the tip of the tallest building, in Insintation, which stands a hundred and seventy-nine thousand and nine hundred and eighty-five feet tall. By this, he managed to land on the building, without getting so badly hurt.

How Zeth managed to get to that direction, when the building was over a hundred miles away from where he was battling the bat, is still a mystery. It was as if, the bat blasted him to be there. The entire tip of the building was the size of three Olympic stadiums, with a goat pentagram being the image. The sounds of the winds were squealing at a very high pitch. Zeth could hear the screeching noises from the bat. He could hear the bats wings flapping louder and louder as he approached him.

Despite the great confidence he had obtained from Nortric, Zeth had a great fear of the bat, knowing that this creature, wasn't even trying at all, in combat against him. And the bat still manages to beat Zeth to a pulp. The bat appears in front of Zeth again, with a small grin on his face, he walked towards the Cat Rat, ready to beat him up some more.

Once more, Zeth ran towards the bat, with a little more caution, and tried to karate chop the bats left hip. The bat grabbed his right arm and kicked him in the privates of Zeth Drastic. Zeth got back up and jogged towards the bat, with an elbow hit aimed to the throat. The bat defended himself against the move, with his left hand. Zeth tried to kick the bat with his left leg, however the bat, blocked it smoothly with his right knee. Zeth administered two punches, from his furthest right and left combos. The bat blocked that well too.

Zeth attempted to get a hold of the bats face, to head-butt him, however the bat was first to head butt Zeth, causing his forehead to bleed. Zeth tried to use, a kangaroo kick, and the bat blocked it with his right thigh. The bat socked Zeth on his Adams apple, and caused the CatRat to gag, and gasp for air. Zeth then tried to do a right kick on the bat's shoulders, the bat blocked Zeth's move perfectly. With Zeth's fist punching the bats chest, Zeth only managed to do one contact punch on the bat's chest. The total number of punches all together was eleven.

It was that single punch that caught the bat off guard. Unfortunately for Zeth, it did not phase the bat in the slightest. The bat screeched at Zeth in a death-defying manner, that put Zeth in a position, of having to cover his ears, to protect his eardrums from damage. Zeth attempted tpo punch the bat, and the bat caught his left arm. The bat karate chopped Zeth's left arm, and by his right thumb knuckle, he hit Zeth in full impact on Zeth's left rib.

The bat did a spinning right foot kick, on Zeth's upper part of his head below his ear. The bat punched Zeth on the left side of his chin, and right side almost immediately. The bat, knee kicked Zeth, in the groin, and upper cut Zeth with a blow sending Zeth forty feet in the air. As Zeth landed on the floor, he still was motivated to get that bat. Thinking about all the many years, he has been struggling taking on all these villains by himself.

Zeth thinks about all of his friends, and his teachers, and how they all influenced him into becoming the man he is now. However, against strong odds, what was the main influence that these people had on him?

"Oh, what was it?" said Zeth.

The bat walks towards him and says, "a cruel joke." The bat raised his left leg, and with a compelling foot drive, he hits Zeth square between the eyes. Zeth smiled at the bat and said "your good at sensing my motivations? And how could you know? Why are my motivations a joke? All the trial has to be is one good while. After that one good while, there doesn't have to be any intention of evil anymore. Sadly, some cannot handle the weight, of sin. With the near endless amount of confliction, upon each other and within yourself. I am beginning to wonder, how you were seeded, being a role model to many. In a social, nihilistic entity. Who knows how fallen you and Eogo really are?"

The bat continued to walk towards Zeth, while Zeth was talking, "one thing is always certain, for that, if you do not follow everything that is good, being something, you turn into evil which is nothing."

Nortric Drastic

Zeth ran towards the bat, with his fists aimed at the bat's abdomen. In order to fake the bat and cause certain surprise, However, the bat blocked that surprise, and attempted to kick Zeth. And an energy duplicate of Zeth, attacked the bat on its back. The energy duplicates only lasted for five seconds, and the bat was not phased in the least.

The bat rose, and punched Zeth on the mouth, and did over ten punches on the right hip. The bat almost punched Zeth with the back of his fist, but luckily Zeth blocks with his right hand, and knee kicked the bat, right smack back in the abdomen, this time releasing a large fume of gas. The bat seemed untouched, turns around smacking Zeth across his right cheek., and elbow slams Zeth between the eyes.

Zeth in less than zero point zero twenty fifths percent of a second, sledge hammers the bottom of the bats chin, and punched his belly, over fifty times in two seconds.

In excitement, the bat kicks Zeth, sending him flying nearly a hundred feet a second. Before Zeth could fall off the cliff, the bat flew behind him kicking Zeth across the back. The bat elbow slams the back of Zeth's neck and stomped him on the back of his head.

Zeth tries to use his backup plan, a device of some sort. However, the bat took it out of his belt and threw it away. The bat flew into the sky and slammed his feet on Zeths back. The bat repeated this over and over, that it caused the surrounding building to shake. And the building begins to crack. Zeth cries out in agony as the bat sinks its nails and feet into Zeth's back, cracking the top of the building a little more. The bat noticed his move and was ready to deliver the final blow. As he was just about to, with dark energy, Zeth rolls to his right, jumped up high, punched the bat's wing and karate chopped the top of bat's head. This caused the anthropromorphic bat to crash down, from the tall building. Zeth managed to land on a room that wasn't destroyed, by the impact of both, the bat and his attack. Zeth walked down the stairs, and the bat appeared in front of him, with Zeth saying.. "you were not even trying were you?"

The bat did three sledge hammer attacks, on Zeth's face. The bat knee kicked Zeth on the hips eight times. The bat punched Zeth on the chin, causing the Kat Rat to fall down the stairs. The bat, raised up, and stomped on Zeth's back, and did an elbow slam with an electrical spike, sticking out of the tip of his wings joint.

Zeth, groaned and moaned, in torment, of the spike, piercing through his back. The bat chomped his venomous veins, into Zeth's belly, and duplicated his head..into several heads… Having more mouth's and teeth to chew on the Cat Rat. Zeth screamed..to the point, as if he were burning in hell. The bat who was fighting him, is the secondary antagonist of the series.

And his name is Caprin.

CHAPTER 2

Crawling

Zeth, the striving Cat Rat, for overcoming the heavy weight of sin, is all alone, with blood all over him. His clothes were torn into pieces, and parts of his skin was chewed off. He should have been dead, yet he wasn't, and for some odd reason, Caprin, was nowhere around.

All Zeth could see, was a large hole in the wall, showing the sky, with the sounds of the winds blowing with a very high pitch in a frequency.

Zeth new, something was strange, and struggled to say these words.

"So…. He came, aaaft, after all." Zeth says, as he was crawling painfully, and was about to attempt to pursue, one of his most difficult challenges.

Zeth emerges and has to descend down the stairs of a skyscraper, which happens to be around one hundred and seventy thousand feet. Every time Zeth tried to descend each stair case, he shaked and tremored as if he was having seizures. The amount of energy that he had to put forth, was like a vehicle being driven with no rubber on rusty old rims. Despite the shape Zeth is in, the achievement of each floor, was not impossible, however the biggest problem was, not managing to reach all the way to the ground. It was instead the worry of other members, of the Insintation…coming to get him. Standing still on the first level of the stairs, Zeth slipped down, and landed his nose on the wall.

"Ow". Said Zeth in a bitter tone. There was another stair level that he had to descend, a level that stood above thousands of levels, that he had to further his journey. There should be no such thing as, to take a nap, for himself, especially under and above these circumstances. By dragging and crawling himself to his left in direction, Zeth was making a trail of blood down the stairs. Remember he had just been beaten by Caprin.

The next staircase that he was carefully descending, felt strange to him. It was as if he was feeling a burning sensation, from the first level, and then a cool breeze came upon him at this second position. Each stair case was pulling him closer, and closer, into throwing his balance off his feet and hands.

Each level of stairs had eighty stair cases, and Zeth was nowhere near the bottom, with his second level that he was positioned. Now, when it comes to using the elevator, Zeth was unable to use it, not only because of how badly hurt he was, it's that the elevators, in the tallest skyscraper on Insination, had pass codes in order to operate them. So, this has made it incredibly difficult to have to sustain moving down the stairs.

Once he reached the sixty fifth staircase, Zeth again loses his balance, begins rolling around the level, and lands on his back. Zeth shrugged his shoulders and continued making his way down the left side again, and began to descend through the third level. As Zeth began going down the third level, something felt different, In both a good and bad way. Zeth's eyes, looked disturbed, and his mouth changed reactions rampantly. Zeth could feel it, and it was not from any outside energy. This feeling was within him, more than just a gut feeling, and he just couldn't understand it.

Zeth, fell for the third time, however it took him only halfway down the staircase as he tumbled, and rolled. Not all the way down the level, like the last time. AS he was carefully trying to maneuver down each case, Zeth could have sworn he heard scratching noises, all around him.

These new sounds made Zeth alert, and yet the unknown made him feel unsettled. At this time Zeth decides to get to the fourth level fast. Turning to his left, the lights in the building began flickering, in sequences of fifteen to thirty second intervals. Zeth caught his breath, after he began panting furiously, so that he could look to his right and his left, to scope out his perimeters.

No one was around. This made Zeth very curious, and unstable for the moment. Was he over reacting? Or is it because of the insatiable encounters or the fact that something, was out there. Descending the fourth level, was like putting 5000 milligrams of melatonin into his symptom. Zeth began feeling drowsy, and for a moment he passes out, and falls asleep, with the front of his body, sliding downwards on the stairs. He was lying on the fifth level, he just gives out, and falls into a deep sleep, or trance. Suddenly out of nowhere, Zeth hears the same female voice that said his name, before he lost the fight with Caprin, says again….. "Zeth". Zeth returns the gesture with a raspy voice and says, "Lincent?"

"Zeth", said Lincent softly. Zeth answers back.. "ok Lincent, you can cut that creepy hallowing sound out. There is no need to call my name like that twice." Not listening to Zeth, Lincent with a course ghoulish sound from deep within says again… "Zzzzeeeethhhh".

"um, uhh, that really isn't an attractive or appealing way to say my name Lincent". Said Zeth.

"ZZZZeeeaaaaathhhhh". Lincent, lashes out with all her vocal response she could muster.

Several Z's and snoozes later Zeth awake and starts again down the stairs. He felt like utter crap, when he awoke, so by now he is angrier, than scared, at this moment in time. However, the fear, is beginning to take over his mind. His eyes opening wider, and his body begins to tingle and shiver as he thinks about what he will face next.

Down the stairs, a faint voice can be heard…. "Zeth". In a thought of dismay, Zeth became horrified of the unknown. Knowing that a false

Lincent could actually get a hold of him.

"Zeth please. You have to believe me" the voice travels and he realizes that this Lincent could be seemingly real. "How can I know it is you? And not some consumed monster of evil? How can I know, when I have heard the unearthed monster in you? How? How!!! Lincent how can I know?" Said Zeth.

"Zeth you might be right, and no one should ever, ever be near the likes of me." said the seemingly real Lincent.

"what are you talking about?" Returns Zeth. "Lincent, answer me please, don't leave me. Everytime I go through so much crap everyday by Eogo and the Insintation. You have become the key to open a door, that unlocks me from the dark. Lincent..Come back! Zeth desperately cries out. Still no answer.

"Lincentttt!!!!!" He exhausts at the top of his now weakened vocals. Through great strain, Zeth struggles to hurry his motion downwards, and says… "I'm not letting you go Lincent! We are going to get out of this..Do you hear me? Just you wait and see this Insintation debacle is going to end very soon. I'm coming for you Lincent hold on!

Finally, as he reaches the sixth level, there was a sixth sense surrounding Zeth, causing an inner panic, raising his bodies adrenalin. And sanity on the outside. Mid way down the sixth level he crawls, and all the lights had been shut down throughout the whole building, so it was move by move downwards. At first his breathing began as a panting, then he built his confidence up and almost spoke again, however despite the boost in confidence, it quickly disappeared into desperation. Knowing, that whatever he was going to face, the chances of him surviving in such a severely injured state, was going to be a unlikely victory for Zeth. And he Knew it too. At this time not being able to see in the dark, Zeth endured unspeakable hardship as he descended. Suddenly… The effervescent light turns on in the emergency boxes.

The lights power sources were at a low, so it was still difficult to see.

Zeth, used this light to follow shadowing and depth to feel his way.

His hands raw and knees aching, each move became more and more impossible.

Reaching for the seventh floor he felt like he was locked in a room with temperatures above a hundred and twenty degrees, the balance in his hands and position made him shake profusely. If Zeth doesn't get to the seventh floor he's going to crash down again. As he reaches the second to last step of the sixth floor, he felt a cold foot, stomp on his fingers. Zeth gasps and falls to the seventh floor, crawling as fast as he could. Zeth made his way to the center of the floor, where the emergency light, and he sat and gasped for air.

As Zeth scoped his perimeter, he noticed except for the emergency lights, and nothing but darkness, that he was in a panic. However, he was not screaming, just freaking out about the unknown. Zeth knew he had to control his emotions. He cannot lose focus now. Then suddenly, pain soared through-out Zeth's wrists, causing him to burst out in torment. It was the venom from Caprins fangs that was coursing in Zeth's body throughout his veins. From yelling to barely breathing, Zeth shakes like someone having seizures. Fading into the darkness, nearly passing out, Zeth knew he had to endure, and become immune to the venom at the same time. Tightening his fist, clinching his teeth, and squirming, the CatRat was in a battle against a disease, that was putting him on the brink of death. The blood cells were turning green and brown causing Zeth to feel fiercely cold while sweating out.

Zeth begins coughing, as if he were in a smoke-filled room, and coughed so much that he began to choke. His legs were moving directional like a snake coiling in and out, and the rest of his body slowed down to almost a stop. Death was coming. All that Zeth could wonder to himself was the actual fact of going down further into the darkness or not. Would it be his solution? Was there ever a huge point in doing all this, fighting the evil?

Is existence, with the highest, truth or illusion, to what we all must put forth? Was the way to avoiding a nihilistic plane all a lie?

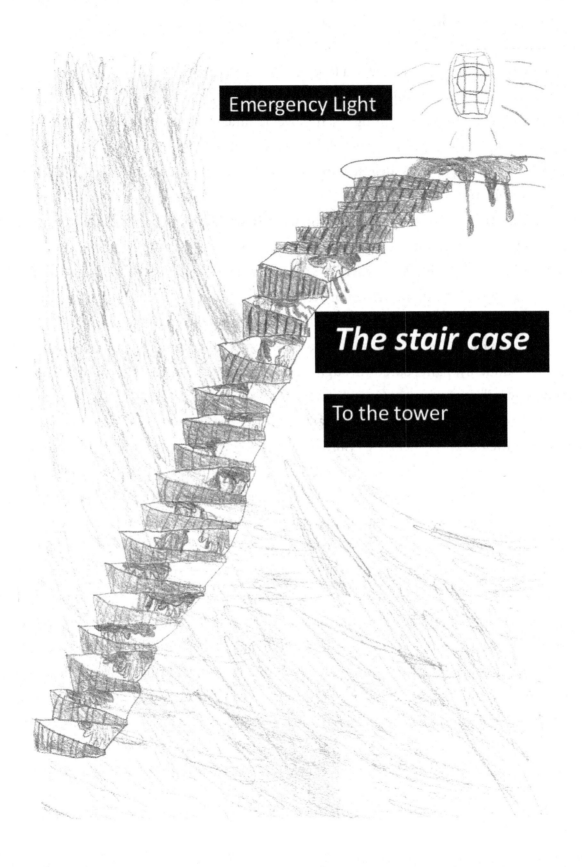

Emergency Light

The stair case

To the tower

Zeth couldn't think anymore, his mind was plummeting down quickly into a master Insinations wants or needs, from their view which is void.

Zeth was enraged by their motives, which actually helped him breathe a little easier. His body moving faster, and his persistence rising higher. Zeth was not giving up. He fought the venom like a child lifting 300 lbs. Zeth growled like a demon possessed woman, grabbed his hair frantically, and cried like a baby, eyes bawling and raining tears.

Slamming his right hand down onto the floor, Zeth's eyes looked like a deranged rabid dog. His voice cracked and gurgled as if cancer had eaten his neck apart. The pulse in his veins had raised so much that his skin looked like inflated runways. The veins on his wrists enlarged to where they were blue shining through pink aura. Everything his eyes saw were bundles of distorted colors, of red, purple, and sometimes light blue. This made Zeth find humor in how he looked, dying. Suddenly he begins laughing like a maniac, he stood up on his feet, and echoed his laughter throughout the whole building.

"Zeth is hallucinating and acting like an overdosed of meth, had hit his system!" Said Zeth, continuing his hysteria. In just a few seconds, Zeth fell on his backside, clenched his teeth, and hissed like a cat. For a while, His skin, was appearing as if large snakes were traveling under his skin. He hears a ringing noise. The noise was so bad, that he closed his eyes, his head moved left and right slowly, and his mouth opened and shut rampantly. More pain arrives for Zeth.

Zeth's hands lose control and start choking himself around the neck. This was the effect of the venom.

Zeth's arms then turns into bear heads, with eagle eyes, and they both say, "plummeting is a treacherous lane to go by, wouldn't you agree?"

Zeth yells back. "Noooooo I do not agree!!!" Zeth takes control of his bear like arms and says "or at least I don't agree with what you're referring to. It's not about falling into darkness, it's the courage to defeat it. Not being of the tearing that it does. Wait...why the hell am I talking to my arms?" He immediately went back to normal. As he continued to feel more pain, from the venom inside him, Germs and microscopic robots were destroying the cells in Zeth's body. This results to crying out blue goo from his eyes. "Is this attack of fire ants gonna stop already!" Said Zeth. Beyond his injuries and pain from the venom, Zeth slams his head, on the floor and knocks himself out. Over twenty seconds of darkness and silence passes, until a female voice that sounded like Lincent, spoke out, and said." What are you doing Zeth? Come out here, and let's enjoy our paradise." In an explosion of light, a beautiful world was shown. It was very colorful, the ponds and skies were crystal clear, there were tons of people playing and singing. It was all perfect, the grass felt like warmth, giving Zeth, comfort and joy. Suddenly! he sees Lincent with a anthropomorphic rabbit child. Zeth smiled, and walked towards them, going to the most fun places, he had ever been to. The rabbit boy, held Zeth's left hand, then held Lincents right hand, and they both swung arms with him. After that, they flew up into the sky, and were fascinated, by all of the creative designs that people were creating with clouds. They went inside a swirling bright yellow energy of a tornado, and unlike most tornadoes, it did not harm them. As they were spinning around and around inside it, all of them said "weeee!"

After having so much fun, they saw a bright gorgeous yellow energy in the sky and raised their hands up into the air praising it. "Isn't this amazing Zeth, how Bill is so happy with what's going on. No more sorrow, no more pain, no more death, we have finally made it to our destination, right?" Said Lincent. Lincent looked to her side and gave a concerned expression, from her face "Zeth, are you okay?"

Said Lincent in a more concerned tone Tears were coming down from Zeth's eyes and as he began to cry out loud, everything around him turned gray, melted, and withered away. A voice was heard in the background that said. "Cringes yah, don't it?" Zeth had heard this voice before, it was from many of the criminals that lived down in the city, of whom he had encountered before. His name is maskcat As Zeth turned around, he could not see him clearly, He appeared bubbly pink with a distorted hallow blur on the apparent head. This appearance was due to the result of the venom that is currently inside Zeth. "Oh no, don't worry, i'm not here to pull any of the things that irritated you in the past, i'm just interested in giving you some insight on what the Insintation does to your soul." Zeth showed a lot of anger in his eyes and Maskcat says "That venom can sure inflame inner wants, it's surely a remarkable sight to behold, they said you might eventually cry over it, not in terms of pain, well maybe sometimes, but on the topic of what your striving for, it could lead you into a burdensome old piece of rukus." Zeth gave a more hateful expression on his face and Maskcat says, "And already it's showing"

Maskcat took a breath and says. "It's for sure a tension that is soft as a subtle flute, and some of us do know very clearly that it is within this very soul in front of me. How could it? Also do you think I'm lying, because if you do, then why are there tears coming down from your eyes, just see it for the story Zeth, and realize that tension of wanting greater is what your soul truly is and what it must be, or better yet, what everyone should be. That green paper, the manageable reminder of the limitations of the boundaries of reality, creates an organism of pressure in our many thoughts that are a craving to steal the working energy out of people. like bad writing for movies as a plain old rip off, one way or another the pressure comes into its manifestation towards the experience of the individual. Strangely enough your corrupt energy thieving boss, throws that green paper away, for what himself? Yes, it is himself, that's just how fat his ego is, pure self only, by refusing the faces of green paper that did not show himself, now cry my word of child buffoonery. It's a great zoom in to his character as well as what we are, we're spawn of the greed master Zeth, I want it all, and you want it all. Of course it's for good intentions, but does he want you to do that? Well he does, though at the same damn time, he doesn't, does that even make sense? I don't think it does, it just raises the stress into wanting to become him, which shows it will end up, doing the first sin. There are clues to this, with a story of zillions of people living in greatness for centuries, until a single implement of a thought returned unto man, which showed our more intriguing side of ourselves. Surely everyone knows. Hell, even people living under a rock, should realize this by now, unless they are so into their own gain. It could be said, that would be the reason why it's never known to the sight of gaining more."

"Money, that unconditional tendency, is something that I burned a long time ago." Said Zeth "Are you screwing with my ears, hardly anyone does that, ever" Said Maskcat" One time there was this rich man who thanked and offered me money, I took it and burned it." Said Zeth "Why?" Said Maskcat. "Because of how it came into our stupendity. We could have had almost anything we wanted, with no payment. Sure, if it weren't for such foolishness, I could have donated money to charity, however that's a scam, full of bull ploppings, and lies, and as generous as it would be to the poor, I've offered a different solution for them to survive. it makes them far better off, then with this dumb thing, that should of have never, have amounted to anything to begin with. Now leave before i beat the crap out of you again." Said Zeth with confidence on his face. In a few seconds Maskcat left and Zeth was back in pain of the poison in him. Unlike the pain he was in before, Zeth was starting to adapt to it. He knew for a fact, that this wasn't the worst Caprin has offered by poisoning people. One shake made Zeths face look as if his very soul was sucked out, and had memorials flow through his mind. Memories of what he had to do in order to go up against the Insintation, being almost restless into becoming a spiritual influence on the hearts of the people. Throughout his years of doing the good he's accomplished, it is not much in comparison of bringing down the bad, that the Insintation have caused. Sending the world into a uncleansed disaster that will end, as hard as a ten mile train falling down from the sky.

Zeth vomited, purple vomit with green stripes, on the floor, and heard a voice of his child self-saying. "Shameful clouds you lousy Cat-rat,

It is a no matter, that makes sure that this no matter, will go for that cracked road. This cat-rat thinks he can leap too." Out of shame, Zeth placed his arms on his face, and made a quiet cry. "And what did I say? It's got the cat-rat, like a bear, feasting on his surrendered humiliation" Said the voice of his child self.

Red Spiderlegs, stabbed Zeths right shoulder, causing him to yell while clenching his teeth. Another Red Spiderleg was coming to Zeth, this one was slower than the others. It twitched I'm a haywire, and made nasty loud popping sounds. Zeth tried to pull the spiderlegs off of his right shoulder, however the Spiderlegs twisted around causing more pain on him. As the Red Spiderleg was halfway there, it had black spider bite wounds on it, with hair sticking out of it. What can Zeth do? He was helpless and felt even more pain coursing down his flesh, with Red Spiderlegs slowly tearing his skin. The Red Spiderleg drilled into Zeths mouth, pulling the inside of his throat. Zeth then heard a unappealing voice saying, "And the showdown has arrived, whores, and assholes, with Zeth getting junked by the most unattractive legs in history." In a flash of a second, Zeth saw a shirt fall, that read Travis Oliver Morrowcain. From downstairs, he saw spirits of neutral minds, until another Red Spiderleg spewed out black energy unto the souls. As Zeth reached out with his arm and tried to give those souls the energy of righteousness, it was greatly overshadowed by the might of the Spiderlegs dark energy. "We shall sin" Said the souls. Bit by bit, Zeth began to tear and claw the Red Spiderlegs that was in his throat.

By managing to claw and tear the first layer of the leg, slug centipedes slithered around the red spider leg in his mouth. With Zeth clawing and tearing the second layer, the sluggish centipedes were five inches away from him. As Zeth attempted to grab the sluggish centipede, roots of the red spider legs that was on his body began to grow, causing a suffering and temporary stun for him.

The sluggish centipedes managed to get ahold of him, and sunk their teeth on his chest, Zeth tried his hardest to tear the third layer, however it was much harder than the previous two, which made it more difficult for him to do. Despite the difficulty Zeth was managing to take pieces off from the third layer and punched the sluggish centipedes on his chest, to their death. As Zeth was almost done getting rid of the third layer, the spirits that he failed to give a righteous mind, channeled evil dark red energy on him, saying "please the frustration, please it!"

At first Zeth gave in, tearing the layer faster and faster, however as he was doing this, he stopped and calmly tore the third layer off.

After the third layer was ripped off, there was a slimy dark green skeletal line that Zeth needed to get rid of.

When he grabbed a hold of it, loud, bad quality sounds, screeched out and acid was about to spew out from the torn spider leg.

Out of the shadows, more red spider legs launched in his mouth and nostrils, causing a nasty itch in his nose. The red spider legs pulled him closer into the shadows, Zeth knew he had to act fast, before he got there. He used the torn spider legs acid to burn the other legs off and tore the torn leg in half, which led him to fall down halfway of the giant skyscraper. He managed to grab ahold of the rail of the stairs. With all his might, Zeth managed to get on the staircase and roll down to the next floor. Breathing heavily and raspy, Zeth coughed some more, and was ready to fall asleep. He just couldn't do it anymore the stress was too much for him to handle and by that he passed out. Out of the darkness appeared a beautiful ocean with skys crystal blue clear. "I thought I got you out of quitting, now look what's happening!" Said Lincent

"What do you mean?" Said Zeth

"Just all the pile of trash thrown on top of you, which makes me, the encourager, encourages you to lift that trash." Said Lincent.

"I don't want to do it." Said Zeth.

"If you don't then that freaky thing will do the worst to your body, do you really want that?" Said Lincent

"By hoping for the freaky thing to get it over with, then yes, I want to be a righteous hero, but this is too much for me to swallow, I've done so much of this that I'm tired of it." Said Zeth

"So am I. However, we have to keep going Zeth, It will pay off, I promise." Said Lincent

"What part of this situation don't you freaken understand, I'm done, I'm freeken done!! no more damn it, no more!" Said Zeth. A storm arrived with Lincent into the depths of the sea. "I'm giving up!" Said Zeth. Despite Zeth saying that, he thought about what he'd be missing, if he did give up. Which would put him into, the conclusive decision, of saving Lincent from drowning. Going down felt like a wild ride. With sharks biting him, squids spewing poison, etc, Zeth still prevailed and saved Lincent from drowning.

Zeth woke up and saw the creature, with red spiderlegs. It stayed positioned infront of Zeth with spiderwebs around it. The creature had a light blue slimy face, with large purple and green striped lips, it had one completely green eye, no pupils, just cornea, it had long brown hair, no eyebrows, and a disfigured cockroach body with torn spider legs.

There in between Zeth and the slimy creature were the souls that Zeth failed to channel his energy on. Zeth had to get up and channel his energy, so that these souls would realize that this creature is plaguing them with perversion. The slimy creature whipped Zeth down on the floor and that just made him more persistent to get back up. Again, the slimy creature whipped him back on the floor and Zeth put forth more effort into getting back up. With the third whipping, Zeth continued to achieve what he was doing. The fourth arrived and that didn't stop Zeth in the slightest. The fifth slammed hard down on his back, he smiled back at the creature and continued trying to get up. The sixth one, was the hardest slamwhip the slimy creature has done to Zeth, and for a while he lay down there, looking quite defeated until he attempted to get up once more. As the slimy creature was about to do the seventh slam whip, Zeth scissor cut ot off with his arms and channeled his arms and channeled his energy on the souls in front of them. The slimy creature made more of its sounds and launched out redder spiderlegs onto his feet and hands.

Zeth still kept using his energy on the souls and the slimy creature used its energy on the souls to live in the hallows of sin, this caused a power struggle between the two, of the souls feeling unsure of the path they should take. Eventually Zeths energy was flickering, and the slimy creature's energy was getting larger. Zeth then had an idea to use for his energy on souls, which is not simply rightious, it was more or so joy, happiness and faith on the souls, which began to turn the tide in the heat of the spiritual battle between Zeth and the slimy creature.

The slimy creature endorsed doubt and sorrow with its energy on the souls and Zeth used joy and grateful energy on the souls. The souls were beginning to see who the real enemy was, and Zeth yelled out. "For hope!"

One last burst of energy exploded out of Zeths hand unto the souls, and by this, they charged unto the slimy creature causing it to let go of Zeth Drastic. Zeth struggling to stand up, says. "I need an aid of energy, please aid me!" A few of the souls went into Zeth which allowed to have enough energy to give one last attack on the slimy creature. Zeth jumped off the rails and said. "Now all aid me!"

As all of the souls went into Zeth he used it all for one huge punch on the slimy creature, going all the way down the giant skyscraper. Finally reaching to the bottom Zeth has defeated the slimy creature. The souls left and the slimy creatures last words were. "When they come from under, the fairwell shall be the family's greetings." Those words were heard many times before with Zeths childhood, a prophecy of horrors, embraced from the complete depraved and warped people who have turned into sickos, Zeth knows it all too well of the worst being yet to come, and he feels quite unsettled into facing it.

Zeth crawled, and thought about what Maskcat was telling him, and wondered about success on how it forms a tendency of over wanting things, and arrived to a conclusion of success. It is not the true cause of evil, it is the view on evil of success that sets the damage in motion, while failure maybe needed once in a while for realization of wrong, in the end with or without failure, the view will always be there, and it is up to the person to go for the path, that they want to go with their own view.

Having a lot of trouble getting up, Zeth felt like he needed at least one night off from this, he could not keep on going with this condition however he's still not going to quit, he just needs a break.

The relief of getting that stress off his shoulders felt very satisfying, however he needed to get out of there, because of the Insintation guards coming in, the guards coming in, the odds would have been overwhelming, even at his best shape, it's still difficult. He has to get out of there now. Crawling as quick as a snake chasing after a rat, Zeth managed to find an opening through the vents, and carefully, slowly, he found a way outside. It was windy outside and Zeth could faint sounds of laser blast and energy. Zeth wondered for a moment of what it was and figured out that help is here. Motivation arose within Zeth. He got back up and looked around.to see where the help was. He heard loud heavy foot stomps.

Zeth's eyes looked a bit tensed, his mouth stern and turned around. Coming to Zeth, they shadowed all over him. The shadow gave the appearance of a huge fat being. The shadow was shown popping the knuckles. Zeth has arrived at a further showdown against unbearable weighted down forces and looked a bit angered at what he was looking at.

CHAPTER 3

Motives Of Savages

A CHILD CAT-RAT ON a pool of dark orange swirl, with green colors, and there up above him was the sun with a black vortex on the center of it. Out of the vortex was a skinless cat-rat, and it grabbed the child. Meanwhile with Lincent. As the female cat-rat jumped forty feet into the air, a heatsinking missile was chasing after her. Lincent ran towards it, and used a device that controlled the missile and aimed it towards the one who shot it at her.

The shooter was a six-foot cyberpunk anthropomorphic redbird, with a reflecting mask, red glowing eyes showing from it. The bird had a black coat with the red goat emblem on the back of it. He also wore black pants that had a belt with equipment on it. The boot-shoes were light weighted but dark in color.

The cyberpunk redbirds name is Drofred and he is the son of Rodsord Septob. The bird dodged the missile and rode his cyberpunk motorcycle, going nearly five hundred miles per hour. Atop a three-thousand-foot skyscraper. He flew up into the air with his motorcycle and flapped his wings in order to reach Lincent. As quick as a jumping spider, Lincent jumped towards Drofred and got a hold of him by her legs on his neck. With the two weapons that size, pie shaped angle of 42 degrees and edges of steel, Lincent started to chop Drofreds shoulders simultaneously before he attempted to hit her with his beak.

With one of the forty-two-degree weapons, on the left side of her neck, Lincent reached to her garter and pulls up a five-inch needle from her right leg and stabbed Drofreds left shoulder into the bone.

Drofred yelled over the puncture in his shoulder, just as Lincent was about to slice his throat, but Drofred dug his right feathered fingers into her mouth, causing Lincent to gag. Lincent then started to grind her teeth on Drofreds fingers, biting the middle, and index ring finger off. Drofred screamed a very loud high pitch and Lincent grabbed a hold of his damaged hand, squeezing it tightly with her right hand. She kept hitting his shoulder extremely fast and kicked Drofreds face. She jumped off the motorcycle, and landed feet first on top of a seven-hundred-foot building.

Meanwhile with the elite Insination in the conference room.

"That family traitor Zeth Drastic, has been a vine of poison ivy to our bloodline for far too long. There will be no greater disgrace than him. Mark my words on steel for that, and I can't believe he keeps his last name, he's against us and yet he keeps something we hold dear, what a sick man!" Said Elargarious the six foot six inches anthropomorphic german eagle.

"As Eogos servant has addressed before, there is no need to stress over, he is just one of a handful of who would dare stand against us. Another reason why, is because Zeth is currently getting his butt whooped as we speak. However, what we should be focusing on, is how to amplify and exploit peoples inner weakness by making them corrupt minded and warped into their own obsessions. Then we elite Insination shall reign dominant minded over the dumbed down masses. Does that sound like a wonderful idea for you Elargarious, making you the superior? minded person above all, in ruling all with an unstoppable fist, with nobody ever challenging you. Your telling yourself, "to get stronger and and weaken them. Aeon blessed Savage and Fa-bast for their grand influence upon us." Said a five-foot six-inch anthropomorphic bird, with a crow body on the left side and dove body on the right, it even has a male and female voice. This birds name is innercist.

"Amen to that," Said an eight-foot three hippopotamus, whose name is Iaintyobuddy. "Cheesy complements, but I get your just not…...."

Before Elargarious could finish his sentence, Caprin crashed down the conference room with everyone in shock, except Innercist. "Don't worry guys, he's just screwing with Zeth, maybe even literally." Said Innercist. Everyone in the conference room laughed their butts off at what

Innercist said in his mind. "Oh Elargarious, like your truly equipped to rule? it's sad that people like you even exist, thinking you can live, like some Greek god ruling all, when we all know that will never last forever. You are nothing more than just a fulfillment of evil trying to be better than good, it's like what they say, if you don't follow everything that is good, being something, you turn into evil of which is nothing. Wait! Was that my thinking for sinful plans? or was that 'him' inside of me? Nah it couldn't be him, he agrees with me, even when I'm off and he is on. He's kewl with me, there's much evidence of him wanting to do what I'm made to do. Aw hell! Do I have to speak to the son of a bitch, to know the truth? or is it a speculation on his face? Come on, it can't be that... and it is not that! It was me knowing what would happen to that tyrannical that is supported, not opposed by me, but of the other soul that's in me, however it's well um, well it's not a mind game, at least I don't think so. Man, this crap is driving me crazy. No, it's not like that, and that's that!"

Meanwhile with Lincent.

"My father and with a great swear from my mouth, shall be avenged." Said Drofred, who ran towards Lincent with a painful punch on her right arm, in defence against Drofreds punch from his left fist. By both Lincents knees, she slammed on each side of Drofreds cheeks, cracking each of the bottom part of his skull by a little bit. With her right elbow, Lincent hit the Adams apple of Drofred, and by her left knee, she hit on the bottom of his testicles. "Mama help me!" Said Drofred in a chipmunk voice. "I killed your mother" Said Lincent, using her small tail, Lincent began to strangle Drofred by his neck, and punched through the helmet mask. Lincent kept beating Drofred senselessly with eyes possessed until she stopped for a moment.

ELARGARIOUS

Drawn by Allen Knox

"Oh no, I shouldn't give in to that darkness, I shouldn't let it take a hold of me, this type of violence is going too far. I'm giving into sin, I've got to go before this gets out of hand." Said Lincent. Drofred punched Lincent on the forehead, and kicked her twenty-seven feet away from him.

"Come on Lincent, beat me till you have nothing left to punch, give in to that darkness you've gobbled up in your soul, and accept transhumanism as man's destiny, it's what Jerico and Savage kept trying to address for so long, please accept his great offer." Said Drofred.

"Transhumanism is arguably what started the whole debacle of evil in the first place. With one thinking, he could ascend greater than the one who was already greater. By becoming a fading spark, away from the almighty flame, into the darkness. One would think it could become everything. It's meant to be something, it is now nothing." Said Lincent.

"Your sitting duck motives, are sickening Lincent, Jerico knew of our potential, that we all could become all-mighty flames. If we get rid of that darn obstacle out of our freaken way, resulting to a never-ending non-struggle. Jerico always tried to address this to uncle Elargarious of the importance of it and its meaning, and better to the point where we will be better, and i'm going to fulfill that, indefinitely." Said Drofred.

"We are limited beings Drofred. and it is only one, who can provide eternal vitality for us to simply exist, because we're all going to eventually wither away someday Drofred. There is only one who can bring us back into existence, and it is to go in the all-mighty flame so that all sheep will not wither away into void, for we are all sheep. Our Shepard is calling for us, and I'm coming home." Said Lincent.

"Those were completely despicable words from a petite girl, of who beat the living crap out of me. oh well I guess you really are a waste of Insintation potential after all." Said Drofred. Drofred pressed a button on the left half of his chest, released a few dozen balls out of his coat, the balls morphed into silver dodo birds with green eyes.

"Tear her flesh, like the savage animals you are!" Said Drofred.

"The more you talk vile, the more you prove my point into why we will never be equipped into becoming the all-mighty flame." Said Lincent

"Just shut up and die already!" Said Drofred.

"This guy seriously needs to be rehabilitated." Said Lincent to herself.

Meanwhile with Zeth

Feeling yet again, and sinking into a void, feeling completely left out and hanging on with his faith for the all-powerful. Continuously having doubts in the fact that he could be of any help at all. If he was of any help to us, in regard to living forever, then why did he say we have to die? When he swore for us to live! There were so many, where Zeths confliction's rosed to constantly having trouble to find reason in that. Questioning why a faithful person has to die, despite the deed being done? This thought process always gave Zeth nightmares. Things he always must keep hanging on to despite evil being destroyed. It still lives. Blood kept pouring around Zeth, with chewing noises in the background.

"On the first day of work you were told what you were looking to be. he's not there, first week, and even millennia. The M(^&%#$& is not there." Said Zeth moving his head extremely fast.

"My mind it's going haywire, what's going on, what's happening, what's stirrrr..stirrrrr.. strung up my nerves." Asked Zeth with a stressed face. Then arms with holes on the wrist, appeared from a bright light and a voice called out and said.

"My sweet child, I have given my entire existence for you, and everyone in the world. As long as you are faithful to me, you will never perish from the Earth. You've got that pumpkin?" Said a mysterious holy male voice.

"Well done Savior, well done." Said the seemingly real Caprin. "Holes on wrist, how lame, I'd prefer to see your head on a pitchfork, your sadist lover!" Said an angry Zeth.

Zeth in a spinning vortex, had his eyes opened wide and said.

"What in the world am I saying and why am I saying it, Caprin you foul monster, you! You? Um who are you? Said a first angry to confused Zeth. The being that appeared before him was named None

The figure was five-foot one inch tall, with arms, rusty, iron legs and a bunch of snakes formed into a goat emblem mask upon the face.

Zeth just didn't look more afraid or mad, just sad. None flew like a witch towards Zeth with a nasty laugh. With one karate chop, Zeth knocked out None on its head and said. "I'm sorry."

Out of nowhere, None grabbed Zeth from behind and licked acid on his neck. Zeth grabbed Nones arms and threw the creature far away from him. Again, out of nowhere, None jumped on Zeth, clawing his face. Zeth threw None far into the sky and started to run far away from None as fast as he could. After a long while of running, Zeth encountered a child eagle, who spoke to a distorted red being, with the child saying.

"So, he is holding us, back right?"

"Yes, my dear child, however he doesn't just hold us back, he governs our mental capabilities. He claimed that he is the perfect soul to make sure we are spiritually healthy in suppressing ourselves. What of that was a lie, straight from a get go. we can, and will become perfectly stable people. Because of this, we are people who can do all, by removing the true small. Like all the ones who desire transhumanism, we must get rid of the corrupt lunatic of which I wish I've never known. For the good, true good that is, and for my magic kingdom that amazes more than what that loser can do."

"We could get endless refreshments until our hearts content, but no, the snob who thinks he's better than everyone else says otherwise and the fury that is within me, rises every day from that.

We need good, better, much better, a good of our endless desires delight, we've got to get rid of him. That madman must be out of the picture entirely, and yes it's not going to be easy, that's for sure, and sometimes I...Ummmm, Well sometimes, oh man. Sometimes. Well, ahh man, I just can't say it, okay here it goes. Oh boy, maybe your too young to hear that story kiddo of what Jerico had to do in order to achieve a power greater than that old tired fossil. No not those people, but someone else. Someone who, well, it's best not to talk about it now, however but what I will talk about is one simple thing. If you can overcome evil of which is nothing, greater than something, then you become good. That is everything, remember that child, remember that." Said the distorted red figure

"Oh, don't worry Savage, I will" Said the eagle child.

A dark sandstorm swarmed on them, making it impossible for Zeth to see though the red clouds forming the word blood.

Then a kid with dark hair, white paint skin, red eyes, cat whiskers, cat ears, mouse tail with rugged clothing and blindfolded was with Nortric.

"You sure about this?" Said Nortric. "As sure as a hamster eating cocaine." Said the child catrat

"A little too much info there, however that's okay, now let's battle Zeth." Said Nortric.

Adult Zeth tried to reach them, and when they clashed, none grabbed Zeths legs and said. "Revenge, It is what needs to be done with you, I must have revenge!" Said None

"I know you want revenge, how could I blame you, we Drastic have a deal with something far much more than evil itself, and I've got to stop it, before it succeeds." Said Zeth.

"Your stains are more than enough to show that you will defeat Eogo. Not since after your great loss against the goat. Doesn't that memory click in? How could it possibly not? You still trying, to forget? Ha, even after another serious reminder by Apinbul. You still want to say to yourself, that never happened. When I'm the living proof for that you are evil, and no matter what you do, you'll never live up to the savior." Said None.

Hatred was shown in Zeths eyes. He was about to kill None with his fingers, however he didn't, and began to walk away.

"Sick freaks like you aren't even worthy of being merciful, because it is something that none of the Drastics belong to, especially you."Said None.

Zeth turned around, looked at None with the most serious face, and says." No matter what good or evil i've done, certain times are only thoughts of knowing what to do when doing true good, and how you go on living, not obsessing." Said Zeth.

"That even reeks more than your evil deed Zeth Drastic." Said None.

"It only reeks because you've failed to understand any situation of what the helpless are pushed into, wearing shoes with spikes in them, instead of comfortable fits, and even despite that, I can't hate you, and I'm not even sure if I'm frustrated with you. It is just more towards me." Said Zeth.

"Hissss!" Said None.

None screamed out loud and jumped with fire flaming on the person's body.

Meanwhile with Lincent

Lincent threw sharp thin needles into the dodo birds. The needles turned red and caused the dodo birds to melt. Drofred pressed a button on his wrist, and a thirty-six-foot creature, climbed up the building and appeared before Lincent.

It had sixteen arms, first one being a crocodile tail. Second a pink lion's claw, third a fiery green skeleton, fourth a deformed human hand, fifth a ten foot back. The sixth with a drill, seven nearly has a monkey's entire body except feet, eight a golden chair on its butt, ninth a shredding machine in between its legs. The tenth an acid organic left hand, eleventh a windmill on its head, thirteenth a body of a clone of Drofred as a partial neck. The fourteenth has the right-hand rainbow colored, fifteenth, snakes, and sixteenth an electric hand on its chest.

It was all just hands and its name is Wasteful and it's made of garbage.

Lincent laughed and said. "That's the funniest thing I have ever seen, who made that, a two-year-old?"

"My daughter actually." Said Drofred.

Seriously?!?! Said Lincent.

"Yes, and she's nine years old, your douchebag, now attack wasteful!"

Said Drofred

In less than ten seconds, Lincent dislocated all sixteen shoulders of wasteful and elbow the center of it, which inside was a brain.

"No way, I don't believe it, that was my daughters best work, no!" Said Drofred.

"Well, it was wasteful." Said Lincent.

"Hush beast, hush, now it's time for my trump card." Said Drofred. "I'd like to see it." Said Lincent.

Drofred ran after Lincent with his fist raised up, ready to punch her.

"Is he really going to do the most stupid and boneheaded move possible? Surely this illogical loser has a trick up his sleeve, right?" Said Lincent. In her mind. Drofred attempted to sock Lincents face, she dodged and blocked a kick with her mind thinking. "No tricks? That's kind of a shocker."

Up in the night sky, bright colors of rainbows were colliding with a shadowy bat figure in the background of Lincent and Drofred fighting.

Greater than a hundred and fifty-million-mile radius, everyone within its reach was being under the power of the 'holy and wicked', By the temptations of evil and the heart of good, all caused by these two in an aggressive battle against each other.

"Great it's that broken forgetful man, who is trying to go against us."

Said Drofred. Lincent tried to punch Drofred, by her right and left fist, however he grabbed both fists, knee kicked her on the belly and said. "And he will always be broken."

As Drofred was about to sledgehammer Lincent with his fist, she kicked his knee so hard that it caused him to fall down. Lincent kept punching him and said. "It's you who's going to be broken, not him, he's better than what this family will ever be, better than you and your father!"

In anger, Drofred grabbed Lincents neck, squeezing it as tight as he could, and he even punched her harder than before.

"You know I hate female aggressors, especially when they mock a great man like my father, of who. Before Drofred could finish his sentence, Lincent threw a needle on his left rib, this caused him to scream and let go of Lincent, giving her enough time to do a karate kick, right on the forehead of Drofred. The needle began to melt in Drofreds left rib, causing even more pain for him.

Lincent was about to deliver the final blow on him, however Drofred was in so much pain that she didn't think he was worth it anymore, and she knew that Zeth needed her help fast.

"Oh no you don't, there's no way your leaving, this is definitely not the end." Said Drofred.

"Um bro, your left rib is melting, I think we need to wait until the next round okay?" Said Lincent.

Drofred pressed another button and something digital began to flash from him. Lincent looked a bit nervous, wondering what he was planning. In a bright blue flash of light, a creepy old lady's voice said. "I am the fully evolved and perfect being."

Meanwhile in a nightmare

Variants of all forms of evil swooped in a 6'11" naked male cat-rat with a eight pack, muscle arm height up to fourteen inches, muscular legs, purple skin, dark eye, blond hair, cat ears, whiskers and mouse tail.

"Well this is quite the most fascinating image here, all of those funny words and thrills implementing in my thoughts. Are they not just the most swell guys, always having a magnificent lingering on me into wanting to be like good ole daddy? And oh boy hasn't it worked? Well that's a good bet that was already successful long ago. And sometimes my wonders in life, make me dwell into a thinking of, was I always on their side? Surely that has to be true right? I mean after all this whole temptation of sin thing, it seems to be inevitable. It's always chomping us by the very seconds of our lives pulling us closer into a purely perfect opposition of our experience, no matter what state you're in, rather being a preacher, sinner, rich man, happy man, or pitiful man, there will always be the coming temptation of evil, of the very just good, it's all a checkerboard box, the whole wretched thing. Blast it, the blast the rotten damn thing straight to Hell! Yes Hell, no the eternity of a tortured one, but the absolute nihilistic ink that covers the entire shred of paper.

Yeah that lovely ink. Aeon blesses it. Oops that poops. Sorry for the blessing guys, I am terribly sorry. Wait!! What about sorry? Should sorry even be mentioned under the circumstances of the coming, the call, the coming, not the call remember. Is that, okay guys? okay...Okay? Alright now let's get back to topic here, the word sorry. Yep, that's something that probably shouldn't even be mentioned because if you're sorry about something, true good will ask you permission to come to your house, and nihilist should never use the delightful non-magic word. Sorry is the one and not only. A summoning of good coming into a nihilistic house, we can't let that happen, yes, it's simple however it's deadly, very deadly. Wait no, urrggghhh, that's not what should be used, it's deadly the greatest necessity of nihilism, or the skin, if you like to call it that anyways, if you don't then, away with you anyways, go eat a milkshake. just keep lusting your delicious disgusting milkshake, until it turns you into a corrupt individual. Indeed, it does that, there's even a document to prove it, milkshake destroys lives and if that's true then of course everything destroys lives, bwaahahahahaa. okay that actually is cheesy, or may have something else, i'm pretty sure it was. Oh, whoopsy daisy, isn't pressure a great persuasion of our enemy's, however first things first, let's make an imitation, yet somehow your convinced he is your despair Sherdumb, he is the sadist of all sadist, if our bodies were supposed to feel pain then why is he asking us to go through it? How cruel, just something that might be a sure must to vomit at. Anyways into the backtracking checkerboard box theory, it's a fine one, it's not opposition of fences, it's more of a verdict of surprising and unrealism. Same time result, it's two of the same needles with the only difference, in the color being red or blue."

Pauses, shrugs, then goes back to ranting.

"PPPffftt haahahaha... that's not only comedy gold, it's comedy ruby and sapphire, haahahahahaaa. Oh boy, that is an amazing, never fails, it always succeeds. let me imitate some red followers. This one is better, it has more energy, blue followers, no this one is better it calms you down, ha ha, you know what this reminds me of? The repuppies and the democats, always growling and hissing, chewing and clawing, It's just like that, yellowdog and yellowcats, there's no jackasses like the donkeys or fat asses like the elephant. It's just the mutt and slut, there is no greater alternative. Quit killing yourself, honestly, with evil being inevitable. Wait and rip that paper into endless shreds. Evil has won before infinity, how could it not be excepted of which should be seen, of that is the reverse of seen. Also did I even mention not-knowing? IQ of negative infinity, a power that's all-greater and not all-greater at the same time. Morality doesn't exist in any world to live in. There is no 50/50, there is no chance, don't escape from it with fiction either, fiction writers or fans of fiction, it's all just an imagination that should never have been a dream. Nightmares are the best dreams, not that one where the supervillain takes over with the real person getting angry, releasing all the superheroes against the antagonist, by the ending of drinking coffee with them or fighting vampires at a food-store or saving a celebrity from intelligent criminals, with an ending being with the celebrity. Giving you're a good train station on impact in between the knees in a secretive agent manner, woah, hold on, that's a sin. The beloved sweet honey tummy fulfilling see what I told yah, all with a fulfilling of coming to falling." Said a strange unknown unstable pack of spiritual energy coming out of the tall cat-rat. By the first few seconds the tall cat-rat shook his head, more than twice the speed of a salt shaker. His head just kept going faster and faster until he said. "Naahhhhaahahaha!" Screamed the cat-rat.

Out of the yin yang sky, formed a mouth coming out to eat him.

"Sam, it's rusty time!" Said the mouth

"I beseech the Depart!!!" I can make my own paths, without brainwashers like you, puzzling my behavioral functionality." Said Sam.

"You will come inside me now Sam." Said the mouth.

"No, I'm not" Said Sam.

"Yes, you are" Said the mouth.

"I'm about to punch the crap out of you and I'm not going in!" Said Sam

"Then I'll make you do it." Said the mouth.

Sam jumped after the mouth, with his fist ready to punch it.

Instead of that happening, Sam was gobbled up, inside a vortex of lunacy.

"I love sin, but I've turned my back. Shouldn't it be forgotten? Should it!?!?!" Said Sam with his body turning into a zigzag distortion, with him saying. "Urgghh the growl and grr of temptation of yah the weak link of a doofus. It's gotta stop, where's the barrier to end this lord? Where is it?!?"

"You will be the true heir of the Drastic family, not the disgraceful one. Said Nortric in the distance.

"I've heard that before. That was a really long time ago." Said Sam. Suddenly appeared, a petite cloaked figure, making a clay of goats.

Sam's head and neck shakes a bit and Sam said. "My mother liked doing that, she was cool, both anti-Drastic and full on Drastic from time to time."

Sam grabbed his face and screamed out loud. "What is going on with me?!?! Why am I behaving so weird? It's this energy, it's corrupting my mind, oh good god, I'm losing my soul, it's like as if my entire existence is drowning into an ocean with no land visible!" Out of nowhere another

DUALISM

SAM

Sam jumped in front of Sam and punched his entire forehead off, killing that Sam in the process. This Sam behaved more silent than the previous, and its eyes focused like an owl with a calmer tone he told me.

"It's about time that a, unstoppable mess like this is thrown in the microwave, would you agree?" Said this new current Sam.

"Yes" Said Nortric walking up towards him. Nortric looked a bit excited seeing Sam and said. "A great Drastic like Sam, should bring a strong psychological persuasion on the minds of any person, it should be govern-mental, an air blowing in a helium balloon, cause the release Sam, make it expand with them, it's endless to infinite usage of implements that feels so, Oh, what's the word for it, loose? No it's not that, it's like a behind your back doing, regardless of it being intentional or past the accountability, it is a done contract signed by a winged beauty."

A pause of silence for a moment happened between the two with Nortric looking very serious on the matter. Sam was smiling with cold eyes staring back.

"The in front, and behind, of expanding flowing energy can circuit my lovely possessor. All that sin needs to do is exterminate all those other Sams out of the way in this imaginary world of his and yours, and once that's done, the Rightious-ful that is now few shall be none, and your making will pain the great beast that will feel the self-inflicting, and payback that will arrive furthermore for that rabid sewage screw over to his torment, unless he likes it, but that's the head start, his defeat will be done and you will set forth in motion of what's going to happen." Said Nortric. "True and in all honesty there's probably not much that can stand in our way, except myself of which shouldn't be myself anymore." Said Sam.

"Spiritual can be poisoned subliminally, physically and a lustful hateful energy, It sends the foundation of an established reality down. Sam you can do it, don't give up, destroy the remaining Sam's that cover this world of yours. The defense mechanism must be purple black you can do it Sam, don't give up!" Sam's eyes looked a bit distraught with the words.

"I will do it" Sam dissolved into a dark purple gray cloud and combined the surroundings of Sam's imaginary world.

A hallow face was shown on Nortric with eyes of sadness.

Meanwhile with Zeth.

Iaintyobuddy the 8'3" hippopotamus giggled as he tossed Zeth into the air, and continued to slam him on the wall with his giant right arm holding Zeths legs.

Iaintyobuddy did the truffle shuffle as a bouncing hit on Zeth, repeatedly for a moment. Iaintyobuddy giggled and said. "My friend is in the circus!"

The giant blew in Zeths mouth, causing the cat-rat to blow out for a while, with Iaintyobuddy trying to do a body slam on Zeth's face but misses and lands on the concrete, cracking it a bit.

Iaintyobuddy giggled a bit and said. "Ga gaa gaa gaaaoosshh!"

Iaintyobuddy picked up Zeth and swallowed him whole.

"Welcome to the new ride, and enjoy your tickets, kind furries!" Said Iaintyobuddy. With another giggle, he played the bongo with his fat belly, and in the stomach of the giant hippopotamus, Zeth was being tackled by moths with very unimpressive torpedoes on their backs.

Iaintyobuddy vomited Zeth, He grew up to 14'2" and said.

"Hippazapdee, I grew to a greater size than you, whooaa yuoouu, fak yah, Zeth if it weren't for a lous like yah, then I shall not inherit kingdom of the kingdom!" Iaintyobuddy giggled even more and said. "See that's where it's all funny, don't yah think it's that I'm a dumbass? well blimy the banana pedaling, I am a dumby!" As Iaintyobuddy was giggling, Zeth punched him on the nose.

"Little kitty, were you cleaning my nose, because I needed it!" Said Iaintyobuddy giggling even louder. Zeth then grabbed a sharp piece of glass from the floor and cut Iaintyobuddys left nostril off.

"Your making me mad" Said Iaintyobuddy, with an unhappy overtone. Both Zeth and Iaintyobuddy stared at each other for a while with a serious look on their faces. Iaintyobuddy giggled some more, raised and moved fingers up and down and said. "Get ready for a disectamee!"

The injured cat-rat hopped away from Iaintyobuddy and managed to continue climbing up a ladder.

As Zeth was climbing up the ladder, Iaintyobuddy climbed behind him while giggling and tried to grab his legs. Zeth managed to avoid that, however Iaintyobuddy tried again and almost succeeded in grabbing his legs.

Zeth was sweating with stress getting to him, and Iaintyobuddy just smiled like a happy camper and continued making baby noises.

With the third try of grabbing Zeths legs, Iaintyobuddy laughed like a baby and then roared.

Finally, by the fourth try, Iaintyobuddy managed to get a hold of Zeths right leg and giggled very happy like. Zeth then kicked Iaintyobuddys right arm, however, the only reaction Iaintyobuddy gave, was him laughing. As Iaintyobuddy was about to drag the cat-rat down, Zeth spat on the hippopotamus eyeball, resulting to him letting go of Zeths leg.

As Zeth climbed up to the top, he picked up a red ford 150 and threw it on the head of Iaintyobuddy, causing the giant hippopotamus to fall down two hundred and forty-five feet.

Iaintyobuddy giggled, rolled around, laughed and said.

"Hhheeeeeeeaaaaaaahhhhhhhhh heit maaaaaaaeeeee!!!!"

"You dumb fat body of a hippo, he's getting away, why the hell didn't you tear down the stupid ladder? You, dumb dodo blob. Oh, wait a second, it's because you are dumb retarded Jackass goof of a terd of a pile of dodo, your head is vomit. You no good for nothing pink ball from the rednecks southern, nutloses brud.! Ich werde deine Verdammten arme kaune! Warum sind die fudgen starken ficks wie diese sind so dumm! FuNken Verdammt noch mal, ich brauche meind cocaine

Hundinnen, ich brauch es! Du weist, verdammt den verdammten familienverrater, I'm gonna eine hure und entspannen, was fur eine schreckliche Nacht das, ohhhh I'm tired, this mouth speech to dumb flips of doo doo licking is tiresome, I just want the power back darn it! Wieviele mal ich habe zu mischen, um es zu bekommen dammm esss!" Screaming loudly!! Anger raging!!!

As Zeth was running away, Elargarious jumped on him continuously kept punching the cat-rat on the face and says. "For all your flippin crap of verdammt! I will be spoonfed no more of hearing such silly notions of eradicating a conquest hungry solipsism ruler like me, I'm not letting that happen, and you will know from the message of sinking in deeper than the bottom of the ocean, you're getting it Zeth, that's for sure, your definitely getting it sonny boy!"

"Let me have some with fairest wheel!" Said Iaintyobuddy.

"No screw you, I'm doing this my way, now buzz off before I cause a huge amount of blood loss on your neck!" Said Elargarious.

"What neck with blood?" Said Iaintyobuddy.

Elargarious looked both stressed and angry and says. "Verdammt hippo, why the heck did anyone think of all the messed-up goofs, from la la toons, would fit for as a initiative Insintation henchmen!? You're just a big fat dumb hippo, ich hasse hippos! Just die hippo and get the heck out of here!" Zeth kicked Elargarious so high that he flew sixty-five in the air.

"Oh no you did not just do that! And to think that Nortric of all people liked being with this asshat and wait a second do you have a grenade on your hand?" Said Elargarious while flying around.

Unknown to Iaintyobuddy, Zeth found a grenade in his waist and waited for the right time to throw it.

Zeth threw it on Iaintyobuddys belly which bounced towards Elargarious. Elargarious dodged most of the blast, though parts of it did hit his right shoulder.

"That was on purpose, you verdammt acid asshole, i'm gonna slice yah up in two, you dickwad!" Said Elargarious with an upset expression

"Well the heck with you too Allygarrious" Said Iaintyobuddy.

Elargarious screamed in anger, dashed at Iaintyobuddy, front flipped and landed inside the giant anthropomorphic hippopotamus mouth.

As he was inside, Elargarious continued to punch the inside of Iaintyobuddy and said. "Verdammt!"

Meanwhile with Lincent.

Lincent wasn't all beaten up from the fight against Drofreds transhumanist form. Its appearance being silver, golden legs, four red wings and green eyes, its speed was much faster than before, combative speed capable of exceeding over a thousand attacks per millisecond.

"You know what, I'm sick of these egotistical snob-bots who brag on and on about their superiority over organics, like just kill me already, your words your words that spewed out jerks like you, just don't shut up worth a Krap, so please If I may ask, shut the heck up." Said Lincent.

"My evolution is far more of……….."

Before transhumanist Drofred could finish his sentence, Lincent yelled out. "Please just shut your trap, and if this world is based on evolution rather than life is utterly meaningless right to the very bottom of it."

Up in the sky, a rainbow light zigzag around and Lincent says "Oh crap he's doing it again."

Lincent jumped, dodged four tornadoes spiked attacks from transhumanist Drofred and leaped with a fist landing on his belly. However, transhumanist Drofred used a metal fist out of his mouth, landed the punch right on her nose, grabbed her throat and threw her on the wall, and says.

"So that's all you were capable of doing, just a leap and a punch, even a professional bodybuilding third degree blackbelt martial artist sometimes has to bring in some extra hits to pull the defeat on their health bars. like what the heck? are you trying to prove, ha ha look at me i'm super cat-rat girl, I can kick butt any day for only a five dollar payment, that's twenty five percent increase in taxes too folks, like are you are playing a children's game with me, because it seems to be out of the alternative of combative application, maybe you're finally starting to realize why Transhumanism is a need for you to beat me, which brings me this."

Transhumanist Drofred threw a small glass plate on Lincent's belly and said. "By the spirit of Savage, the ox, you will accept Transhumanism and deny the dictator of whom you shall not ever swear allegiance to again, oh by the way we're winning the influence on the people, from the past present, and a guaranteed future added with it too."

Lincent looked a bit confused and said. "Um didn't the past go downhill with every one of whom Savage was influencing?"

"Never mind that blowup from that freakishly unlikely outcome and see through the stupendous goal of power, sure we may have get off the rails, but in good time we'll soon achieve perfection in becoming all-powerful, my uncle Elargarious is kind of into the solipsism view of things, so that might be a controversy, however that can be fixed. No biggy, he just needs to be more of a member not a singular entity, that's all." Said Drofred while giving a stern look at Lincent and said.

"Want to see a recording?"

Lincent looked a bit surprised and said. "Are you for real?"

"I'll take that as a yes" Said Drofred.

A hologram appeared inf ront of Lincent that showed Jerico preaching to the people.

"Nightmares only happen If you don't follow your dreams. And anything great can happen my friends. It's all a good result, in never getting old cycle. My magic is not a small world, it's a world of wonders, and full of magic. Sadly, there are some people of whom think i'm a liar and call me blasphemous, and full of deception. Although you, my fellow followers, know that you are not fooled, they are the ones who are fooled. Poor them, the fools that had the common sense from within to know better and just kept screwing everything up like babies tearing bed sheds. Like all of us in the sake of honesty, the rise above the cage master, must be accomplished and must do of what shall be done."

BLACK VORTEX HURRICANE

THEM US AND WHY?

WHILE VIEWING GOD AS A SADIST

CAPRIN

Clapping and cheers roared loudly in the hologram, and tramshumanist Drofred turned it off and said," The ultimate hear what you want to hear, and I don't care if people do fail at it, for that through hard work and determination, nothing is impossible.

"Said a guy who killed over millions of people." Said Lincent running and crashing down through a glass window that was close by her.

Transhumanist Drofred blasted lasers on the building of the lasers, causing the building to fall down.

"Stubborn shill" Said Drofred.

Meanwhile high into the sky at 11:24 pm, a dark energy of the the size of vy canis majoris behaved like a hurricane with fiery sparks shooting out of it, that were hotter than a heliocentric sun. Inside the center of it, was a shadowy figure who used dark energy on the city, however there was a beam of light bursting out like a supernova, rivaling the shadowy figures dark energy on the city.

Everything that was good was combating against evil, that was for nothing, of many possibilities of thoughts upon the people.

The rivaled energy was so close in power, that everyone was behaving neutral, however there was a sudden shift from time to time with this clash. The people were acting crazy and then extremely calm, in certain places in the city.

The one who was blasting the dark energy is Caprin, with his strength not as suppressed as it was against Zeth. Caprin raised his billion-ton sword and began to charge with it to the bright figure who was beginning to struggle, battling against Caprin.

The question is who is this person, is he some chosen one figure, antihero, or some unlikely hobo who got zapped deus ex machina?

Whoever this person is, It must not be a friend of Caprin, and is his enemy.

End of chapter

CHAPTER 4

Catch The Cat Rat

1959, FEBRUARY 9TH 7:45 AM

In the wilderness of the trees, there were two anthropomorphic characters speaking to each other. "Our good manipulations on that loser in serving for the Judgmisspast has worked well right Garotaro?" Said a skinny 6'4 anthropomorphic horse.

"Well to be real with you Ezall, such doings have brought forth dominance on the world before. You have just got to be very sinister in doing so." Said the fat 5'5 anthropomorphic lizard Garotaro.

"She promised us the lust of many virgins, right?" Said Ezall

"Yes, the Judgmisspast did say that, she also said that this wimp is destined to be with Lincent, for God knows why. It is what it is, and at least we're getting something really good in return from it." Said Garotaro.

"True that Garotaro" Said Ezall. "And you want to know something strange, she said we would be under perpetuated torment by asking any question about it. Don't you find that odd Ezall? How she would want that to be so secretive? We all know she doesn't keep her mouth shut on many things and yet she wants the information unknown to quite possibly everybody, and that is odd." Said Garotaro.

"Meh, I don't care, I just want women" Said Ezall.

"Me too, and who knows, maybe that weakling might be made a legend out of us, or maybe he'll just end up like the rest of the idiot youngsters who believe in our lies." Said Garotaro, with an evil laugh bursting out of him. Ezall did the same with his laugh as well. Then a completely white painted skinned anthropomorphic character arrived with a mouse tail, cat ears, whiskers and had large dark shaggy hair, that covered his eyes, and Garotaro says. "Did you get her?"

The shaggy dark-haired person nodded and Garotaro says. "Fantastic now, show me where she is. "It was Lincent strapped, by a rope all around her, and had duct tape sealing her mouth.

"Well done Zeth, I knew we could count on you for the schemes, and for that, you get to have a real good time with her." Said Ezall.

Zeth looked at Lincent with eyes of a soulless serial killer.

Lincent tried her best to speak through the duct tape and all that was heard was mumbling.

"Take off those pants boy, we want a good stimulating, porno from this, so make it good." Said Garotaro.

Seeing the look on Lincents eyes, Zeth was shaking in fear, It was if he knew it was wrong, but couldn't understand why.

"Is this why we brought this moron here, I thought we we're going to become real good teachers to you, like what the hell are you doing? This is your chance to show whose boss of that town, by dishonoring miss goody two shoes, and if you won't do it then darn it I'll make the penetration in her." Said Garotaro.

Lincent looked at Zeth, with eyes of fear and concern, while gently turning his head right and left.

This gave an unsettled and confused look on Zeths face, with him closing his eyes, and his face tightened over what decision to make of this. "You know what, screw this, waiting garbage, I am going to explode!" Said Garotaro, as he pushed Zeth aside and looked at Lincent like a pirate opening a treasure box.

"Don't forget me, hahaahaaaahaaaa!" Said Ezall.

Garotaro grabbed Lincents cheeks, with an analysis on her face and grinned with insanity flowing in his eyes and said. "This is going to be one of the best days of my life."

Quickly with his rusty dagger Zeth sliced Garotaros throat, and nearly killed Ezall. However, it was only a slight stab to his chest.

"You freaken waste of filth, get over here!" Said Ezall, coming after Zeth.

Zeth, stabbed Ezalls left eyeball pulling it out with his rusty dagger and plucked out his right eyeball with his left fingers.

Ezall grabbed Zeth by the face, and he punctured the skinny horses face with his dagger which caused him to scream up to high heavens.

"Son of a cursed seed, curse you, curse YAAOOUUU!!!" Said Ezall, in a berserk state of frenzy.

Zeth tried to pick up Lincent, however since he struggles to lift fifty pounds by both his arms, he decided to untie her instead.

They both got away from there fast and took a stop on a dead tree branch. With Lincents duct tape off, Zeth looked uncomfortable sitting next to her.

He turned his head away looking at the stars, while Lincent looked a bit pissed at him.

Zeths curiosity over what Lincent was thinking about this whole mess was full of cringe shown on his face and was unsure to turn his head at all in seeing her reaction to all of this.

Eventually Zeth did turn to see Lincent, and she was right next to him. They both stared at each other. Lincent looked aggravated and maddened. Zeth was looking like he was about to poop in his pants.

"Why did you change your mind?" Said Lincent.

With eyes opened wide, Zeth took a deep breath and said. "Boobies haahaa weeeeee!" Zeth ran away while spanking his butt, and with disappointment shown on her face, Lincent says. "Real mature."

1959, March 24th 10:40 AM

In an average town, lives a twenty-five-year-old Cat-rat named Sam Drastic, who influences souls in spirit form against the sinful influences that are for the Insintation.

"No anger but peace and well thinking" Said Sam while his bright pierced energy into the minds of the people in spirit form.

And then a shadowy figure said. "He's convincing them against sin, we must retaliate!"

A group of shadowy figures charged their dark energy onto the people. "Accept your inequities, crave nonstop eating, want more, troll and spam like a spastic autistic child. You will become lusting for flesh, break free from those miserable chains that are called holy, and you will be free!" Said the shadowy figure whose appearance was beginning to show that of a cat-rat.

The people started to have a little more of dark explosive energy, the kind of energy that indicates, that they are accepting sin as "the normal".

"Overcome the serpents' words, it's not worth it, for that true greatness, is to withstand such offers for the real treasure ahead, which is peaceful and balanced minded." Said Sam with bright energy bursting out of his hands onto the people, which was beginning to change their energy from darkness to light.

"That's not gonna happen Sam, I'm going to overwhelm these people with my army of darkness, and they will, accept sin!" Said a shadowy figure whose appearance was fully shown, a cat-rat with a pirate hat, black and white striped t-shirt and black pants.

"Aren't you supposed to be more specific on that, like more focused on Jerico's way of doing it? not all out? but more about gaining power, and not use all spiritual temptations? Am I right, or are you running out of ideas Kalo?" Said Sam with his energy getting brighter.

"I'm not running out of ideas for 'god ascension', I'm just making them more rebellious that's all." Said Kalo with her energy flickering out.

"Yeah, that's for sure 'the notice' isn't it? Jerico wanting to use depravity as a tactic to influence everyone into the mindset, of becoming greater than the all-powerful blasphemy type of nonsense, you're an outdated enemy Kalo! When we find your vessel, it's gonna go night night." Said Sam.

Suddenly! The energy of the people turned dark again, and Kalo says,

"Shouldn't have rubbed in an ego of that pathetic spirit of yours! All that bragging weakened those meaningless spiritual powers, and now the acceptance is coming into Jericos Drastics goal. All to become over going into power, and defeat that gut-wrenching power in the clouds, I win!"

"I will save these people, good must triumph over evil, and you will succeed Kalo." Said Sam, with more energy coming out of him.

"That strain is not going to work even within spirit form willpower has its limits and yours is showing, arise darkness, arise!" Said Kalo using her dark flickering energy that was having longer gaps on being absent in usage. "Darkness, don't you fail me now, corrupt their minds and stop running out!" Said Kalo in distress, however her spiritual dark was giving out fast and many other members that were supporting from behind are gone.

"My allies of sin, where have they gone, were they killed behind my back, like the heck happened?!?!" Said Kalo, with even more distress in the spiritual battle with Sam.

Through strong excitement Sam released a ton of bright yellow energy unto Kalos energy, making her struggle even further against his powers. "Uraagghhhh, this is not happening, their supposed to sin damn it, no!" Said Kalo, being defeated by Sam's powerful spiritual energy.

"Kalo we've given you so many chances to stop what you were doing for the past months and now you must be vanquished once and for all."

Said Sam with his energy still flowing around him. The reason why is because of him, not letting his inner dark tendencies get the better of him.

"You snob jerks must have killed my teams' physical bodies, but this isn't over, I'll be back, and when I return, you and the whole damned town will pay, I swear it!" Said Kalo.

"How will it pay, when your initiative for such doing's is conflicted?"

Said Sam. "You don't know anything from that, I'm not conflicted in helping out dad, I'll always be there for him every step of a way!" Said an angry Kalo exploding with red dark energy.

As Sam was beaming his energy towards her, he says. "In the end, you know what kind of man he really is, don't you Kalo?" "Just..Just go away!"

After she said that, Kalo immediately left. Sam looked at the people in spirit form and smiled with complete happiness on her face. He was so glad that he had accomplished influencing their hearts, into remaining good and not evil. It was what Sam wanted for the world and hopes that it will happen very soon, with righteousness and holy delight throughout all within the firmament.

"Yeah right," Said Jerico, in the background sending his dark energy onto Sam, creating a near impossible internal struggle within his mind.

"Those people are easy to influence, and should definitely be loving my offering unto them, and you will eventually agree too." Said Jerico, sending energy unto that Sam, previously influenced, into staying good.

"This temptation, this burden, I must resist it, this must not be any acceptance, god ascension is...A lie!" Said Sam, in a mind struggle under Jericos spiritual energy.

"Accept" Said Jerico, using one simple word with energy into convincing Sam and the people to his side. The people easily reconsidered Jericos motives and fully became covered with dark energy all over them.

"Oh, the power of Sam is full of neat potential and he knows I'm speaking the truth." Said Jerico, amplifying Sams thoughts to extremely high standards into accepting what Jerico wants to accomplish.

"I... Guess." Said Sam looking like he's about to mentally have an un-chain reaction.

"Yes, my nephew, yes indeed" Said Jerico.

"Pick on someone your own level Jerico!" Said an elderly female voice using very bright energy onto Sam and the people.

"Well it's about time, isn't it Pakpao?" Said Jerico. Said Pakpao sending a colossal of energy to Sam and the people.

"Nah, you're just a manipulated sheeple, we can perfect our incorruptions, no one is going to stoop to that decision, we will be perfectly all powerful with no treachery shown in a man's heart, you'll see and admit your wrong and I am right." Said Jerico, while rivaling Pakpaos energy

"And what happened to the ones who believed in that motive, where are they are?" Said Pakpao, who is continuously using her energy against Jerico.

Both stared at each other for a moment with a serious expression on their face and Pakpao said. "Dead!"

Jerico looked disgusted at her statement, for a long time in the man's life, he stayed in a mindset of ascension for a long time, accepting it as a fact of reality and Pakpao giving that one word was like saying a racial profane word to an African.

"I don't have time for this nonsense, we'll get better, and it will be forever!" Said a bit more frustrated Jerico, losing focus with his energy.

"Which equals never." Said Pakpao, who is slowly beginning to dominate Jerico with her energy on Sam and the people.

"A Sheppard must not lead precious children into a mountain with a volcano on top, everyone should know they would die trying, with buried thoughts of knowing they'll never survive lava." Said Pakpao.

"You're such a senile old hag aren't you? These souls are mine Pakpao, mine!" Said Jerico blasting darkness out of his hands.

"People should be grateful with what the all-powerful has offered, and not let their greed destroy them, for that greed is the annihilation of the lords hope, joy and love." Said Pakpao, with her energy convincing the people once into not giving into blasphemy.

"Lies, all lies from a Pigwitch, you should be banished for saying such cruel dishonest behavior, curse your name Pakpao, and curse your doings, I hope you have fourth degree cancer." Said Jerico, with flaming red dark energy swirling around him. Out of the enormous bright figure appeared an elderly redbird named Pakpao with farmer clothing, height 5'4", and its age is past a century.

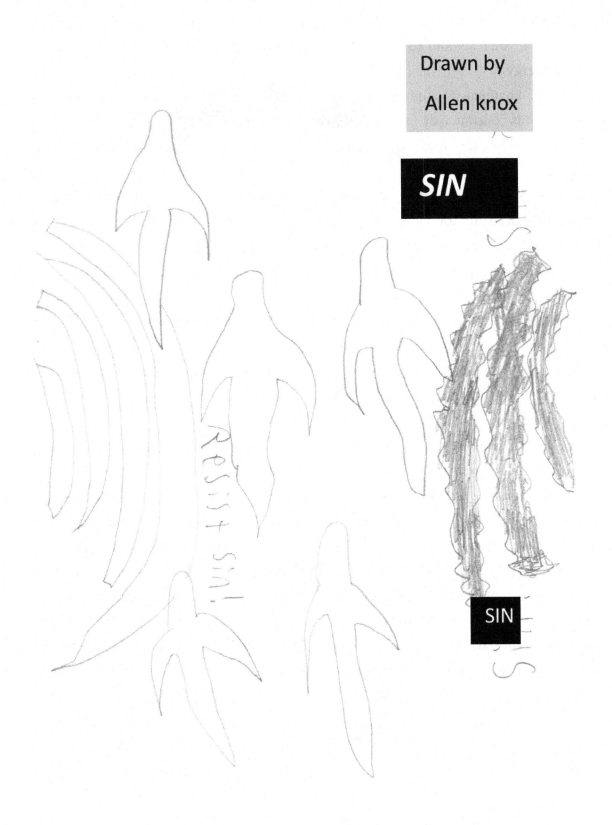

"The mother of the priest wrodsord, and a master Rightiousful wants to challenge Jerico the Drastic. That will guide lives to what a Rightiousful should be, not like those squander level like the master rightiousful, this town will be against the tortures masters evil reign and will succeed!" Said Jerico, shooting out more energy from himself.

"Fools who strive for such false success always get bitten right on the rear end, even if success was done chaos would be inevitable of the certain individuals whom take more than the fair percentage of balance in power, It's as undeniable as a whore out of nearly everyone desiring sex, you can't sustain that Jerico and it will crumble bricks being stacked up, and it's one that will always end up hurting us. We have got to put this to a stop Jerico! Because if we don't the worse will be yet to come." Said Pakpao sending a colossal of energy to Sam and the people.

"Nah, you're just a manipulated sheeple, we can perfect our incorruptions, no one is going to stoop to that decision, we will be perfectly all powerful with no treachery shown in a man's heart, you'll see and admit your wrong and I am right." Said Jerico, while rivaling Pakpaos energy

"And what happened to the ones who believed in that motive, where are they are?" Said Pakpao, who is continuously using her energy against Jerico.

Both stared at each other for a moment with a serious expression on their face and Pakpao said. "Dead!"

Jerico looked disgusted at her statement, for a long time in the man's life, he stayed in a mindset of ascension for a long time, accepting it as a fact of reality and Pakpao giving that one word was like saying a racial profane word to an African.

"I don't have time for this nonsense, we'll get better, and it will be forever!" Said a bit more frustrated Jerico, losing focus with his energy.

"Which equals never." Said Pakpao, who is slowly beginning to dominate Jerico with her energy on Sam and the people.

"A Sheppard must not lead precious children into a mountain with a volcano on top, everyone should know they would die trying, with buried thoughts of knowing they'll never survive lava." Said Pakpao.

"Your such a senile old hag aren't you? These souls are mine Pakpao, mine!" Said Jerico blasting darkness out of his hands.

"People should be grateful with what the all-powerful has offered, and not let their greed destroy them, for that greed is the annihilation of the lords hope, joy and love." Said Pakpao, with her energy convincing the people once into not giving into blasphemy.

"Lies, all lies from a Pigwitch, you should be banished for saying such cruel dishonest behavior, curse your name Pakpao, and curse your doings, I hope you have fourth degree cancer." Said Jerico, with flaming red dark energy swirling around him.

"Blue, thinks of blue everybody's." Said Pakpao, releasing blue yellow energy out of her hands unto Sam and the people.

"I'm not letting you have them! You, you masked faced witch. People forget the 'not meant to do' and a 'do your own existence', is a meant to do!" Said Jerico, while using more dark energy unto Sam and the people.

Pakpao facepalmed herself and then used more of her energy. She says. "We were created by a being who was infinity years before our time, and made us differently than him, not the same, we have all that we could ever want, such unnecessary jealously I see in you Jerico, and these people must not fall for your foolishness anymore."

Pakpao completely convinced the people into accepting who they are and denied blasphemy all the way.

"Well fudge, I guess I've got to focus on Sam now, don't I?" Said Jerico, looking disappointed.

"Do you really think i'm going to let you do that?" Said Pakpao.

"Like, as if, there's anything you can do about it. He was the easiest to influence. I'm opening a door for my nephew, it's no fool's gold, the real deal is here, and I'm getting very close to showing where it lurks around. It's not in the shadows, it's in the light." Said Jerico, overwhelming Sam with his energy.

Sam's hands were shaking, and tail a bit twitching, and face looking cold as ice. The Cat-rat then appeared afraid, looked at both Jerico and Pakpao and said. "I. Shouldn't, be interested in such dangerous goals. A future like that, might end me."

While using her energy on Sam, Pakpaos eyes opened wide and said.

"It will end you, it's always resulted to that verdict, please acknowledge the examples as proof Sam, you know this is true, you know it."

Slowly Sam turned his body to see Pakpao until Jerico used his energy and said. "Remember that checkerboard box theory you made, how the red and blue, the Repuppy and the Democat, the good and evil being no different from each other, however I have a solution that good will triumph over evil, and eternity of better, will be ours forever and Ever. Just white checkerboard and that's the picture."

Gray energy was flowing around Sam, with bubbles of black bursting and popping out of it. Sam looked down with a face of reject, eyes closed, and fist clenched. He looked at

Jerico with a face of hatred and said in a serious tone. "I think that's how I see his defeat in that way?"

Jerico looked a bit disturbed then confused and said. "What are you talking about, my goal is to defeat a should have been loser, isn't that what you want?"

Immediately after Jerico finished speaking, Pakpao using more of her energy on him, says. "Sam, please let that wickedness go, refuse it!"

Sam closed his eyes for a moment, thinking about the two sides that are conflicting him, but for different reasons that Jerico fails to understand, he later then opened his eyes and spoke. "Both of these people are right in some areas, and wrong with the others." Said Sam, with gray energy getting larger. "Jerico does not need to accomplish his goal, however he fails to see the picture of it, and it is..." Said Sam with an uncomfortable pause.

"What is it!?!?" Said Jerico, sounding a bit frustrated.

"I've..I..I've gotta go" Said Sam, with his voice breaking.

"No, you need to listen well, you're being lied to, don't fear becoming an ascending master, it is a yes that cannot be discredited, join the Insintation Sam, you won't regret it!" Said Jerico, using more dark energy on Sam.

"God-ascension isn't your dark motive, is it Sam." Said Pakpao using some of her energy on him. Sams spirit flew back into his body, which is in his room, he grabbed his hair tightly and had a short fuse of a panic attack added to it.

"Oh Sam" Said Pakpao with concerned expression shown on her eyes.

"Meh, he's just distraught over the stress you put him through, and I'll make sure that won't happen again, farewell." Said Jerico, with his spirit flying away.

8:40 PM Pakpao in physical form, looked at Sam on his bed, supposedly resting until she said. "I know your awake, and you don't have to get out of bed, however what needs to be said is the checkerboard can be overcome Sam, it's just an exaggeration of people on fear porn, there's no need to worry about it, okay?" Sam nodded and just before Pakpao closed the door, she says. "Good night"

Meanwhile with Jerico

"Just can't ascend high enough can you Kalo?" Said Jerico, looking disappointed

"I.. was..ju..just doing what was necessary dad." Said Kalo, choking up with her eyes looking nervous.

Jerico walked towards Nalo, and stared down at her, with an unhappy look and said. "Why would the daughter of Jerico Walt Drastic, my own daughter plays dirty like that? We are only supposed to be on a certain Insintation goal, it is to become greater and not let any corrupts downgrade us. We are not meant for revolting hideous ways. We are the future of good, not bringing mindless dumbed down twisted views on the world, do I make my statement known for you Kalo, or do I have to be more engaging with it."

Kalo almost looked fed up with what her father was telling her and says. "No dad, you don't."

"This insulted goal can be done, and you'll see in time that this will be true." Said Jerico.

"Okay" Said Kalo.

When Kalo went into her room, she thought about what her father had told her, with a learning process of thinking.

"What a hypocrite. Him doing such sins to have a gift of power greater from Eogo. I'm not sure if I should be in this darned magic sinkhole anymore. Being manipulated by that goat and Nortric, implementing his words of influence on him, of how we are left out by our supposed true father. He who desires to see more of our suffering, would rather be at peace going out the window. However, I still love my dad, I just don't think I can stay here anymore, he's not the father of who was great to look up to, he's become surrounded with this fairytale of defeating the unbeatable, we can't beat him, and the worst part about it, dad thinks it's possible, oh what am I going to do with him?"

Kalo moaned, groaned, and sat on her chair and said to herself.

"I'm gonna do one more, just one more, and if it fails, I'm leaving."

Meanwhile in the throne of Jerico, where he sits on a ruby chair, with a emerald triangle behind him, and in front of him one of his black armoured 6'10 knights …. "My lord." Said the black armoured knight.

"Yes" Said Jerico.

"A letter from Fa-bast" Said the knight, humbly holding the letter in front of Jerico.

"Oh crap, here we go again" Said Jerico, looking both bored and grumpy, opening the seal, of the letter and reads.

'Dear, which is not so dear, Jerico. My message here, is how unfathomable your idea of sharing all-powerful capabilities to others is. It is not that it's only contradicting, it's also foolish. Only one can have it! There is no such thing as two all powerful, just one, and your missing out on the self-greatness of it. The actual thinking of you wanting to help others reach such levels of power will bite you! That's why I choose for self-love and it's going compassionately well, so far. Very few are agonizing me, and I'm having the good life. All these babes, dominance, and pleasure is all for me, and I'll never let anyone take that from me, especially by idiots like you.'

After Jerico read that message, he walks to his knight and says.

"Double your efforts in battle against the Fabast soldiers. We have a responsibility of morality, to pressure that dictator, and you are going to make it happen!" The knight gave a gentle bow and says. "Yes sir."

Meanwhile in a town that looks medieval, and Scottish. Having very green grass, blue skies, Scottish looking houses, and a few castles. Stood Lincent with a black tee shirt and pants. She was in a room, speaking to Pakpao and Marion Crewl, a 5'3 anthropomorphic female panther, with a blue shirt and black pants.

"You do need to find him! That guy has been disrespecting the town of Toccurapy for far too long and needs to be brought to justice." Said Marion

"I recommend he be watched by Lincent and Sam at all times and learn to behave better than what he is now." Said Pakpao.

"Jail or prison should be the answer Pakpao." Said Marion.

"But the only crimes he has committed which are minor, mind you, are only indecent exposure, a few harassments, and vandalism. He has never killed or hurt anyone, which is why I think he should be taught more appropriate ways of being more of a social person." Said Pakpao, sounding very sure of herself.

"Trust us Marion, we've got this." Said Lincent.

Marion looked a bit unsure with them, wanting to do this, and arrived to her own decision.

"Very well, just make sure he's not doing it again." Lincent cheered in joy with Pakpao saying in a happy overtone.

"Wonderful!" Immediately after she said that, Lincent in excitement says. "We won't let you down Marion!"

Meanwhile outside in Toccurapy, Zeth with his long shaggy dark hair that covered his eyes and nose, and had skin as white as paint, with a mouse tail. He was vandalizing the houses, with vandal words being read such as 'Lick a nugget sucha!'

Zeth clapped, jumped up and down and said. "Hee hee heeeeee!"

Zeth was doing more than just vandalism, he held his private parts and said. "Honk honnk!"

With even more graffiti added to it, he drew naked butts and said.

"There's your bride losers!"

With a fourth row of vandalism, that read 'stupid head, peanut brained, junky, filthy, sluggars. He kept making this graffiti all over the house. Zeth hopped around with one leg and said. "Zipee zipee zipee zipee zzzzuuuupppiiipeeeeee!"

"I've found you!" Said Lincent, running after Zeth from behind.

Zeth turned around looking at Lincent, pointing at her and says.

"Haaahaahahahahahahaahahahezzhaahahahaha titties!"

Zeth then shook his head with his eyes showing madness, he throws a thin four-inch thick tree limb at Lincent, she dodges it well and Zeth tries to escape while crawling like a dog.

"Spam, spam, fashionable looker, trolololololololo, you can't catch me!" Said Zeth, moving away with both his hands and legs on the ground helping him move forward.

"Get over here you are a trolling jerk!" Said Lincent, running after him.

"Suck my golf balls!" Said Zeth, while flipping two middle fingers in front of Lincent. Zeth threw a smoke bomb on Lincents face and she managed to dodge it.

"For months this guy has been vandalizing this entire village, however for some reason he saved my life and I'm not sure why." Said Lincent to herself.

"WA-BAAAAMM!" Said Zeth, smacking Lincents butt and having a shock to the palm of his hand.

"You freaken perv! Said Lincent, attempting to punch Zeth in the nose, however it didn't affect him because he had face armor to protect him.

"Happy birthday!" Said Zeth, throwing cake on Lincents face.

"Urrggghhh, you rotten pest!" Said a pissed off Lincent.

"Trolololololololo!..Oh crap, I ate the beans!" Said Zeth, looking a bit unsettled. "The beeeaaaannss!"

Out of Zeths butthole came the nastiest smell, that Lincent has had in her nostrils.

"What the heck did you!?!" Lincent, couldn't finish what she was about to say because of her nausea, which is due to the horrendous smell that is Zeths gas.

"Ew you vomited, that's not sexy at all." Said Zeth.

"You rotten brat, i'm going to get you!" Said Lincent.

Zeth showed his tongue closely infront of Lincent to annoy her some more, but instead she grabbed his tongue and started pulling it.

"Ow!" Said Zeth.

"Yeah ow, now you're coming with me, and you and I are going to have some serious work together." Said Lincent, while holding Zeths tongue.

"Yah ean ucking?" Said Zeth, trying to speak with his tongue being pulled by Lincent. Lincent pulled Zeths tongue even further with him saying. "Ow ow ow!"

Lincent had, had the last straw pulled on her, and says. "No, I am going to help you with your problems, make a new man of you, and less of a repulsive troll, do you understand?"

Zeth bit Lincents hand, and she screamed at a very high pitch to the pain of it.

"I don't have any problems, screw your teachings and screw this town." Zeth took off his clothes, even his armoured underwear and acted perverted infront of Lincent.

"Hahahahahahaha! Trollolololololo, spam spam spam spam, sweaty lustaarrr, douche bag Trololololololo!" Said Zeth, as he was running away from Lincent. In front of him was another cat-rat, who is Sam.

"So, this is my disgusting cousin Zeth and he's nothing more than crap on an unfinished toilet." Said Sam.

"Have a taste of the devil!" Said Zeth, doing the horn symbol with his hands, pointing towards Sam.

"Feel the desire to sin, inside your spirit? Give in to all of it, lust on Lincents hot body!" Said Zeth, using his energy out of his hands unto Sam. Sam raised his right hand releasing more energy from him saying.

"Act more retarded."

Zeth looked more paranoid and says. "Feell it!! Fffeeelll fffffaaaeeeellllll!!!! Many more will sin sin, sin, sin! Hey what the flip are you doing to me? I amplify peoples spirits not you!" Said Zeth.

"You don't even know the basics of human psychology to do that Zeth." Said Sam.

"Fidget poop, I am the influence of the universe, your just an endurance. Now sin!" Said Zeth.

Both energies of the two Drastics, crashed into each other. However, Sams power was superior and he says. "Go crazy."

Zeth looked more deranged than ever, his face blood red, teeth clenched, fingers twitched, and tail bent, he was angry. Zeth was going on and on with his foul mouth, his entire body was turning red, due to his anger being amplified by Sams spiritual influence.

"GET OVER HERE!!!!" Said Zeth, attempting to attack Sam with a rusty dagger.

"DIE YOU, YYYOOUUUUU!!!" Said an out of control Zeth.

Sam sighed and karate chopped his dagger in half.

"Eat my dirty socks!" Said Zeth, trying to punch Sam on the privates. Sam fell down on the ground, crying like a baby.

"What took you so long?" Said Lincent.

"My bloodline is what took me so long, it's almost going completely nowhere, I just came back here from the spiritual battle with my other cousin and I'm starting to lose hope in redeeming any corrupt minded Drastic. This one is more of an immature jerk, than a high-level selfish person." Said Sam.

"Well we managed to get a hold of one Drastic, that's at least some hope for what we can accomplish." Said Lincent.

"Yeah and he's not even a soldier of them, or even an educated one either, he barely learned anything from our bloodline. But I suppose he's a good restart for what we needs to achieve." Said Sam.

"Just you wait Sam, we will rehabilitate him, and when we do, the step up will arrive for the masses to be redeemed." Said Lincent.

"I'm not going to learn your crap, even if my soul depended on it!" After Zeth said those words, both Sam and Lincent knocked him out on the head at the same time.

1959 March 25th 9:20 AM

Zeth was locked in a garage with Sam and Lincent and he yelled out.

"You're a worthless piece of!" Before Zeth could say any more words, Lincent spanked him on the butt and says. "No cursing!"

Zeth looked infuriated, then angry and says. "Darn you, I can say whatever I wa--!" Again, Zeth couldn't finish his sentence, as Sam kept spanking him on the butt with Zeth growling like a badger.

"Just you wait Sam, when I get out of here, I'm gonna rip your face off!" Sam grinned behind Zeth and whispered. "I hope your mind is ready for discipline."

Though Zeths eyes widened in fear of that statement, his shown teeth looked ready to eat both Sam and Lincent.

"Now, what we're going to do with you is summed up in one word, rehabilitation." Said Lincent.

"The reboobation, doesn't sound like it's gonna do anything for my needs, you're just trying to make me laugh at idiotic teaching, that's all." Said Zeth.

Lincents mouth cringed for a moment, then rolled her eyes and said.

"Let's continue"

Zeths eyes slanted with fist tightened and says. "Let's not!"

Lincent gave a look of dissatisfaction, she looked at Sam for a moment with a face showing disbelief and looked at Zeth like a crime lord ready to kill his wife who was caught cheating on him.

"This is going to be a nightmare to succeed in helping you." Said Lincent. Sam nodded, and Zeth looked excited over this, he knew this was getting on her nerves and continues doing this, with lots of enjoyment out of it.

"Hahahahahahahaaa, you guys are such sucky suckesh losers, I bet your parents regretted giving birth to you!" Said Zeth.

Lincent slapped Zeth on the cheeks, looked at him with a mean face, and determined eyes.

"Never insult my parents again." Said Lincent, sounding very mad but not angry. Zeth looked down with both guilt and shame on his face, and knew he was going too far with the words he was saying to Lincent.

"Now you're going to obey us or there will be consequences, are we clear?" Said Lincent, in a serious tone.

Zeth didn't look at Lincent, because of the shame he was going through at the moment, then Lincent said in a angrier tone. "ARE WE CLEAR!?!"

Quickly Zeth nodded at Lincent and she says. "Good, now let's continue with our lessons."

Boredom was showing On Zeths face. Lincent brought out a chalkboard, writing on it and looked very sure of herself in doing it.

"Our first lesson is going to be about being more appropriate, you need to stop handling yourself, have better manners and eat more delicately." Said Lincent.

"Fine, let's just get this crap over with, and I'll be on my way."

Said Zeth with a bitter look and tone. Lincent looked at Zeth like a nazi interrogating a deceitful jew and says. "Not exactly, this is going to take a lot of patience and I need you to be cooperative with me" Zeth looked like he was going to puke. He hated hearing every word out of Lincent and would claw his face for a day to get away from her, he just hated it.

"Urrggh!" Said a frustrated Zeth.

"Urgh, indeed, now let's begin." Said Lincent.

CHAPTER 5

The Walls Of Jerico

KALO LOOKED A little saddened, knowing that her father was going too far with his actions. She knows she must get out of there. However, she needs to play it safe, until she can escape.

There was a knock on Kalos door, and she rushed to the door to see who the person was, it was her sister Helena Nalo Drastic, who had the same skin as hers. With cat ears, red eyes, long brown hair, red and black striped shirt, black pants, and she is 5'2".

"I know what I'm doing, dad will see what I'm capable of, and this will be a flawless mission for me, right sis?" Said Kalo, while smiling like a child getting ice cream.

"Kalo, even if you had the help of Pellar Dark IX, you won't be much of a threat to Sam, or Pakpao, just get help from my team, and we will finish this in no time." Said Helena.

"Nah, I can handle this, all I need to do is take down Pakpao and her students. I will influence the people in believing Jerico and bring Sam to him." Said Kalo, appearing confident.

"Okay then, and remember, if the people deny this choice of power, kill them!" Said Helena.

"Will do Helena, but I do, I've got a question, I'd like to ask?" Said Kalo.

"What's the question?" Asked Helena.

"Any suspicions that one of your allies could be a traitor?" Said Kalo.

"If you were referring to that fat squirrel, then no, she's just a bit inconsistent into staying on track, that's all." Said Helena.

Twenty minutes later.

Jerico, before entering the hallway to where Helena was, found he couldn't go there for some reason. Jerico kept panting and sweating at the sight of her.

Jerico gave the face of a rabid bear, just looking at her for a second, made him cringe in terror. His right eye opened wide, left eye slanted, teeth shown, nose twitching, hands and legs moving like as if he was frozen in ice, and his tail zigzagged while twitching.

Looking at Helena, caused an alarm within Jerico Walt Drastic! The feeling was a tampering in the nervous system of his chest. Another feeling came crashing in on Jerico, this time it felt like a thousand-foot wall of concrete fell down on him.

Jerico took a squat in the posture of a frog, pulling his ears. He stood up and let go to open the door all the way.

As Jerico opened the door, and was walking down the stairs, he completely changed his insane facial expression. He was looking completely normal. However, behind that look, was a man 'out of control, possessed madman, who seems ready to go ballistic in front of Helena.

Standing right in front of Helena, Jerico took the longest second of his life, to evaluate her, he saw vivid and blurry images of Helena as a baby, remaining in a peaceful position in the cradle. Suddenly! the light that appeared flickered, as Helena began to cry.

When the light disapeared, Helena cried out louder, and a monster with red muscular hands took her! What was heard in the background was Helena screaming in pain like wounded soldier, with the last word being heard "Blood".

Returning from the imagination of Jerico, and into reality of them standing in front of each other. Jerico knew he had to speak to the degree and, at least appear normal.

"So, you think your sister can handle this?" Said Jerico trying his best to hide his emotions in every way possible. Well she thinks so, which could lead to the possibility of her doing it. However, I am still worried for my sister, and the more I see her In a battle against everyone, is the more I see her putting herself in danger, especially alone." Said Helena.

One of the early prototypes of the bird baby that destroyed mountains larger than mount Everest.

— 6 foott

BIRD BABY

Drawn by

Allen knox

S.D.E.

Special destruction of Everest

"You shouldn't worry Helena. She ...she'll be alright. If her life is in jeopardy, I'll send in the Bird Baby, and pull off a genocide on that place." Said Jerico, struggling to not let his inner emotions come out of him.

"That piece of crap is busted dad. When it was nuked by an explosion that could easily blow up Mount Everest. It became rusty, and imperfect. How is that going to defend Kalo?" Said Helena.

"Even damaged, the Bird Baby can wreck, those blind eyed torn zombies, and it hardly ever fails. Remember those battles, of the Bird Baby in its damaged state? How it killed over 10,000 samurai's who's worth is decades of training. In less than two minutes. It made Fa-bast as mad as a badger. I can only imagine what that thing could do if it were fully repaired." Said Jerico.

"And, why haven't we fully repaired it?" Said Helena.

"Because we can't reach that stupid, crazy, lumpy, loony Carl Drastic who does this crazy junk all the time, and you know why." Said Jerico.

"Then why don't you just use Savage, and get him, or her, or whatever that thing is and bring him here to repair it." Said Helena.

Jerico gasped! Briefly. Then released the emotions that he had chained within himself. He then saw a red distorted ox behind Helena, with it seemingly shaking the castle.

"What now Savage!?!" Said Jerico, beginning to look crazy

"Dad, what's going on?" Said Helena, giving the look of being creeped out by her father.

"I want his blood Jerico, I want his blood!" Said the distorted red figure whose name is Savage

"You'll get it when I'm desperate, right now I've got other things to do. So get lost!" Said Jerico, showing his widen eyes, and mouth as he lost control, with the upper part moving up and down, and the bottom zigzagging right and left.

"Like with Helena as a new born infant?" Said Savage.

"Don't mention her!" Said Jerico. As his eyes elongated from their sockets, like a cartoon character.

Helena disappeared.

Jerico, was seeing dead fetuses all around him, engulfed with the color blue as their appearance.

Savage roared! The sight of Jerico, almost made him pee in his pants.

"HHHEEEELLLEENNAAA!!!" Said Jerico, as he bellows out!! All of his emotions, were screeching like a baby pig, being bathed in acid.

"Just, release me! I'll bring forth the blood upon Fabast." Said Savage

Jerico, in a twisted position. He looked at Savage like a minion and started to shake like a freezing naked man in ice water.

"I can handle Fabast with my army alone. Besides i'm saving you for someone else." Said Jerico, gaining more confidence as he responds to Savage.

"Oh, come on Jerico, you know Fabast is too powerful to be alive. After all, he's the other one that Eogo handed the power too." Said Savage.

"I am aware of that, but I need you for the real big fish we are going to fry, not some lesser self-want-it-all idiot. You know darn well, who we're saving your power for!" Said Jerico.

"No! This will be done my way, your too weak Jerico Walt Drastic. I am the top dog! Gaining power is senseless, when you're not choosing the right decisions. I'm taking over!" Said Savage as he runs after Jerico with his distorted arms, and hands reaching out to grab him. "You're not going to take control of me like the last time. I will ascend higher, and do it, by having complete control over you!" Said Jerico raising his hands in a pose of defensive martial arts.

"BLOOD!" Said Savage, as he was grabbing a hold of Jerico.

Both held each other's arms tightly with their energy of red and black, swirling around the two figures. Savage, kept getting the upper hand over Jerico, overpowering him with his energy.

Jerico, saw many strange things on the red distorted body of Savage. He saw a white, short haired naked woman, with red eyes, dark nose, cat ears, whiskers a mouse tail, and she has a pregnant belly.

The woman looked at Jerico and let an anthropomorphic bat that looked like Caprin claw her belly. The word that was scratched onto her belly read 'Vulnerable incest'.

"NNNAAOOOOHHH!!!" Said Jerico, struggling to not let Savage take control of him.

The belly, began to bleed from the claw marks, with a shadowy distorted finger sticking out of it. The woman smiled, as if someone was opening a Christmas present. The belly tore open, showing long arms and legs that stretched out with no end in sight. Jerico screamed in terror at what he saw, while Savage held on tightly to him, making sure he didn't run away.

The body of the legs was an egg, that hatched showing a skeletal female figure that was growing skin. Jerico looked at it with tremendous fear within him. The skin was growing around the neck of the skeletal figure and the figure looked like it was being strangled and being dragged up into the sky. Above Jerico and Savage, was the ceiling transforming into a hypnotizing reptile eye. Savage grabbed Jerico's hand, forcing him to look at the transformed ceiling, and as he was looking at it, in panic and terror of the sight of it.

"Mother!" Said Jerico in a upset state.

"That was you're doing Jerico, if you didn't do it, i wouldn't have existed, and you've done a lot more sins than just that, remember this?" Said Savage.

The reptile eye beamed a laser at Jerico's forehead, causing him to screech in agony from the force of power.

"Helena!" Said Jerico, almost losing his voice.

"Now how about another amplification on your mind." Said Savage.

"No more!" Said Jerico, still phased.

"This is necessary Jerico. If you could release me for at least one week, I could break through the damage power of being infinitely above any dimension of the Hilbert spaces. Just think about what I'm capable of in a short time, unlike Fabast, who's lazier than a sloth. I get things done." Said Savage.

Strangely Jerico's arms begin to melt also with Savages distorted red hands, turning into a lava eruption.

Jerico is now yelling and screaming in pain, with Savage melting even more parts of his body.

"We all know who the true ascended master is here. I thank you for giving me the opportunity in surpassing you." Said Savage, while nearly destroying Jerico.

Jerico looked angrily at Savage! Slowly he was overpowering Savage with his arms, melting the arms of the distorted red figure.

"That will never happen!" Said Jerico, as he was defeating Savage.

Savage roared in rage at Jerico! Eventually Savage melted into a flat rock. However, that rock, and everything else that surrounded Jerico, disappeared. All that was around him was back to normal, without hardly anytime passing. However, Helena was right in front of him, looking a bit weirded out. "We never can have a normal conversation with each other can we dad?" Said Helena, sounding disappointed.

For the first time Jerico looked at Helena, with a face that looked somewhat abnormal. At first, Jerico wasn't sure what to say with Helena walking away from him.

"Helena waits!" Said Jerico, who managed to speak to her again.

"I'm not waiting" Said Helena, walking away from him.

"I'll speak better, I promise!" Said Jerico.

Before Helena walked away from the sight of Jerico, she threw a chair at him, and it managed to hit him. However, Jerico didn't seem affected by this at all and staired at Helena with the same disturbing expression on his face. As Helena walked to her room, she put her face into green pillow and screamed as loud as she possibly could.

"The stench, that is in between my legs, has been a mark since my very young childhood. That disgusting sperm vessel that was left in me. I should never have been scared to leave him! I should have stayed with Sam, not that low life monster! He tainted me, ruined my soul and put creatures in my body that obey him. If I leave now, I'll be in a long period of hurt. I have to stay here, there is no choice! I am in the matter, I am doomed under his whim. I hate him!" Said Helena to herself.

Meanwhile with Jerico.

"My lord, your nephews have arrived." Said the black armored knight.

"Good, now bring them to me." Said Jerico.

Five minutes later, two Drastic brothers appeared in front of Jerico. The one on the left was Rebberus Drastic, who had curly dark hair, dark eyes, black skin, red nose, rat whiskers, cat ears and a rat's tail, that wore a red tuxedo shirt, with white pants.

The one on the right was named Jefferson Drastic, with short dark hair, dark eyes, cat ears, cat whiskers, skin as white as paint, a mouse tail and wore brown pants, and a brown tee shirt.

"So how are my favorite children of Nortric doing? starting with Jefferson." Said Jerico.

"I don't think I want to talk about it." Said Jefferson.

"Give me a good reason why." Said Jerico.

"Because people might see me as a freak for telling you." Said Jefferson, sounding a bit nervous.

"Well! People already see me as a freak, with my motives. That's not stopping me from bragging on and on about it, believe me, I've seen real freaks Jefferson, remember the Judgmisspast?" Said Jerico.

"Why did you mention that foul vulgar woman. We already know who she is, nothing more than a junkyard of nasty, that's what she is. But I get what your trying to say, and to be honest, Jeffersons way of thinking is nowhere near as bad, so he shouldn't be afraid to tell you what's going on, right Jeff?" Said Rebberus.

"auuuuggghhh! I suppose so," Said Jefferson with an unsure over tone

"Then tell me" Said Jerico.

"Well you see, I've been welcoming myself to that. Nothing is around me." Said Jefferson.

"What does that mean?" Asked Jerico, looking confused.

"It means, I have an acceptance on things, that people consider to be more self-destructive, than Fabasts view on the world." Said Jefferson.

"And what is that?" Said Jerico.

"Solipsism," Said Jefferson.

"Oh, I see, you have the path of Fabast within in your soul, don't you?" Said Jerico. "No, and unlike Jerico I don't wish to see my creations as disposable junk ready to be thrown in the garbage. As my children, okay maybe not the Judgmisspast, that, that was a terrible mistake to create something like her, and I apologize for creating her. However as for many of mine, they will be family of mine, and they will never corrupt me into the darkness alone. Insanity of being alone, for that I know my place and it is love throughout the world of my works that I've humbled myself into." Said Jefferson, who looked proud of himself over what he had said. Even if it makes little sense.

"I guess you have a point, however you do believe you are some -power greater than anyone else, which is on the borderline of being like Fabast, but I'll let it slide for now." Said Jerico. Jerico looked at Rebberus with curiosity, and badly wants to know more about him.

"So, how are you immortal Rebberus? because some of those stories of people destroying your body, you always end up with your being back to what you were, how?" Said Jerico.

"A magician never tells his secrets, especially when Eogo doesn't want you to know." Said Rebberus.

"Are you serious on that matter Rebberus? did Eogo really give you that clarification?" Said Jerico. Rebberus took something out of his pocket with both Jefferson and Jerico looking a bit confused at what he was about to show.

It was a letter signed with Eogos blood, that read 'His surveillance shall monitor the continued existence. The lives of all within, are all through creation, with only the consuming of the Under. That is the agreement of this contract.'

Drawn by
Allen Knox

In her samples of teachings, the Judgmisspast caused Carl to have a liking to the Judgmisspast.

The cause was in pre-1959

"What Eogo wants me to do, is to do what is stated, to inevitably consume all except a certain rejected brother of yours, am I correct?" Said Rebberus.

"Fools like this nephew of mine, have no idea of who their dealing with. I am more scared of overpowering Eogo, than I am in overpowering the guy on the clouds. Does he even know what that goat's motive is about? Or does he think by taking the risk that I took with the dark Lord would be a smart move to make? Even Fabast fears Eogo Ali Tainter, everyone I've known, even the bravest of men tremble at the even a brief thought of the master Insintation. Rebberus better know what he's doing in the future with this deal, especially when the most powerful Insintation is involved with it." Said Jerico to himself, while taking a while to process what Rebberus showed him.

"Well?" Said Rebberus, who looked a bit impatient with Jerico thinking about this. "Can you do me a favor?" Said Jerico.

"That answer, is a little bit out of the nowhere, but what is the favor?" Said Rebberus.

"Don't ever mention him again!" Exclaimed Jerico.

"Look I don't like him either, but If I'm going to mention someone, then I better not have any childish remarks from me doing it, okay?" Said Rebberus.

Jerico had a disgusted face and directed his face at Rebberus. It was like as if he was ready to spit out some nasty flemulous goo at him and showed a more ill looking appearance of his eyes.

"He has stooped very low Rebberus, so low in fact that I'm actually considering of being in denial of it. He has no place known to us, except by one possible word that is disgrace, and nothing else." Jerico replied with an ill sounding voice.

Both Jefferson and Rebberus, looked weirded out by their uncle Jerico, and had no idea what to say to him. All they could think about in their minds were one thing. Loony uncle.

Meanwhile with Zeth, Sam and Lincent in a Irish home.

"Haircuts sucks!" Proclaimed Zeth yelling out loud.

"Shut up Zeth, you're getting your darn haircut." Said Sam.

"There it is, he said a bad word, A BAD WORD!" Said Zeth while pointing at Sam

"Please just shut your darn mouth please!" Yelled Lincent.

"Wow, and I thought you were the girl that doesn't say bad words, boy was I wrong." Said Zeth, while looking like he had just won a battle.

"Just get the haircut already!" Said both Sam and Lincent in agreement.

"Alright! Alright, alright, alright already" Said Zeth! speaking really fast.

"I'll do it okay, I'm alright, yah happy now?" Zeth speaking at a normal speed.

"I can't wait for you to meet David, he's an excellent mechanic and really good at giving haircuts." Said Lincent

"Great another member of the evil warden." Said Zeth, while giving the look of exhaustion.

"Not just any member, he's my son." Lincent proclaims.

"Your what!?!" Said a surprised Zeth.

"That's right, his name is David Charles, who is the son of Lincent. Kairi Moore and Sebastian Charles also. David is four and a half years old." Said Lincent.

"I bet he's programmed to do your bidding, and what does this David kid look like anyways? some bird? Cat? Rat? A weasel, like one of my forms." Said Zeth.

"That beginning part was disrespectful! Don't do it again, the David appearance is a surprise. Believe me it's something that's too good to be spoiled. What do you mean by a weasel being one of your forms?"

Said Lincent. In a few seconds, Zeths entire body changed into an anthropomorphic weasel, wearing the same clothes as before.

"Cool" Said an impressed Sam.

"Seriously?" Said Lincent. Quickly Zeth turned back and nodded back at Lincent, letting her know that he was telling the truth.

"You've brolen out one of those weird experiments, haven't you Zeth?" Sam replies.

"And it's all thanks to Carl" Said Zeth.

"Well it can't be that bad, it's not like he ruined your body or anything on the matter, right?" Said Lincent. "He caused a disability on my body, that makes me more limited in strength and speed, I always get a huge strain in trying to, and it's by Carl that the chances for me to overcome this physical disability is unlikely, and never in over two decades of my life have I been able to succeed in overcoming it, I'm a loser and always will be." Said Zeth.

"I don't see you as a loser, I really do believe in you, David has a disability as well in figuring out basic things, but that doesn't mean he's giving up, and has made really good achievements at age four and a half. He has been an inspiration to many disabled people, and I know you can do it, Zeth, I just know it." Enters Lincent who sounded quite sure of herself.

"Yeah, sure I can." Said a sarcastic Zeth.

Twenty-five minutes later All three, Zeth, Sam and Lincent were at a barbershop, with four mirrors, four seats in the room, ten chairs to wait in line, fortunately for them, there was no line to wait for.

A 6'1" anthropomorphic female zebra named Quinn Pryoh, she has blue eyes, wears a red dress, and was three a half foot in front of them.

"So how is the mechanics going with David?" Said Lincent.

"It has some struggles, but David is determined to bust his rabbit tail into making the right gadgets." Said Quinn.

"Rabbit tail?" Said a shocked Zeth.

"And who might you be?" Said Quinn.

"Never mind that, why the bloody devil does that kid have a rabbit tail, is he some freak of nature or something along the lines of that, like what's going on?" Said Zeth.

Quinn looked annoyed at Zeths disrespectful behavior towards her, Sam facepalmed and Lincent sighed over Zeths response.

"Please forgive this poor ole chap. He's just learning his baby steps, sensitive thing he is, that he most sure is." Said Lincent using a British accent.

As a short moment of silence was between the four, Quinn snickered, then laughed and Sam and Lincent began to laugh to. Zeth just gave a bitter expression on his face and felt insulted by the three laughing about his response.

"Does anyone know why?" Said Zeth.

"Why what?" Said Lincent.

"Why does he have a rabbit's tail, is it because of the father, or something out of the norm? Because I want answers, now." Said a serious Zeth.

"It's because I'm special." Said a anthropomorphic rabbit, who wore a black mask that only masked his left eye, with stitches around it to make it stay on his face. And he wore a black tee shirt and black pants. Everything else of this child's full appearance, was what an anthropomorphic rabbit would look like. Rabbit ears down, white fur, and red eyes and this child is David.

"Yeah this is an odd little sperm failure. It's undeniably a crazy womans delivered seed. I feel so bad for you, so broken, and I bet you don't even realize it, how sad I am. Maybe I should be the teacher here, since your mother didn't do a good job raising you? How about I become the replacement for teaching command here, and you people should know that the all-in favor of no objections is coming to me, right guys?" Said Zeth.

David looked confused for a while, then sad, and ran downstairs.

Lincents face was red mad at what Zeth had said. She grabbed him by the shirt and slammed him on the glass window. "I have had it up to the very top with your smartass mouth, you."

Zeth interrupted Lincent with his words saying. "Had enough? I'm just getting started with the party, and there's no stopping me from doing it. My doings are the 'do thou wilt' I don't care about what anyone would think of me, this is just pure funfest. Getting y'all pissed should last an eternity, and i just love seeing your limits being pushed, it's what I find very arousing about you."

Lincent grabbed a pair of scissors and seemed like she was about ready to cut his head off with it. "Lincent calm down! We'll get Pakpao to deal with this, there's no need to get violent" Said Sam using his energy on Lincent. "I think it's better we get the mayor" Said Quinn who appeared a bit scared. "Please don't" Said Sam, who gave a serious tone saying it. Zeth spat in Lincents eyes, which gave him the opportunity to get away from her. As he was, he attempted to walk down, but Sam managed to grab him, and Lincent looked very angry at what Zeth had done.

"Hey dweeb! Are you really gonna cry like the little crap you are? Your pathetic, you should just give up, and be living the wonderful world of the Judgmisspast, she'll make it a paradise for Ya, am I right dweeb? AM I RIGHT? TELL ME YOU FILTHY MAGGOT SPERM RODENT!" Said an out of control Zeth.

"When will yah give it a rest Zeth?" Asked Sam looking at Zeth with the face being ready to beat him up.

"When will you face the reality of the picture of our family, that apples always stay sour and never stay preserved, it's all a bunch of fairy tale lies, and you know it too, remember?" Said Zeth with his eyes staring directly at Sam. "I'm past that view, the world that's created by our maker never intends for it, and I will blind myself no more by that view that can easily be forgotten." Said Sam while staring directly at Zeth.

"Easily? Like that's ever going to be confirmed true, even in Heaven that's not going to be true, and in time, Sam you will reconsider my statement, I swear it." Said Zeth in bitter hateful tone. Sam didn't say a single word to Zeth, everything was silent between them. They were looking at each other as dead on rivals, and they both knew that there's a good chance that there's going to be a serious rivalry in their future clashing their energies against each other. They just know it.

As the door to the barbershop opened, Pakpao walked in with a fed-up expression shown on her eyes and looked ready to use her own powers on Zeth. "You want to fight bring it old hag, I'm ready!" Said Zeth while trying to get out of Sams arms.

"Let him go Sam, this one is mine." Said Pakpao. Without question Sam let go of Zeth, and Pakpao showed no fear in her eyes at Zeth Drastic and looked ready for any offence that he was about to pull. "Lay that fist on me!" Said Pakpao. With rage Zeth was appearing to be ready to punch Pakpao on the beak, and as he was right in front of her, he hesitated, and showed a frustrated face.

"What's the matter? Are you going to beat me up or what!?!" Said Zeth raising his right fist, but not using it for attack. Pakpao stared into Zeths eyes, tapped his forehead with her right feathery hand, and the two were in a bright blue place that looked like a clear sky.

"Get messy with me and beat my body into a million pieces!" Said an outraged Zeth. Pakpao didn't say or do anything, just stared at him with a simple expression on her eyes.

"Do it!" Said Zeth, who sounded very upset and a bit sad at the same time. Not saying anything Pakpao still looked at Zeth, and this made Zeth show his teeth in anger at her, however despite this behavior he didn't attack her at all.

"You think this play's with my brain? Is that what this is about, inflaming my emotions into a depraved jerk? What's the goal here hag, what is it!?! Said a loud Zeth.

"No matter what, I'm gonna remain the same and be a strong perversion among the public, even if there's no one around, I'll still do it anywhere I please. You people can't contain me, my ways will go on forever and no one's gonna stop me. Got it hag? Did you open the envelope already? It says, 'I don't give a pig shat for your indoctrination', and I seriously don't give a shat for these demands, that stupid whore Lincent probably can't even take care of a bastard sperm loser of a child that David is. Who knows maybe she's just a drunk slutty skank who did the bulldoze with someone like me to pop that child 'that no pedophile wants' to be popped out like a gumball machine, as a matter of fact that's too generous, because that vortex is from a monster like her, and by knowing that, it's most likely worse than eating slugs from a vomited sewer. She's just a fool, an idiot, filthy pee brain, stupid head, shatface, deuce bag of a cat-rat. Forget about my sexual interests in her, because Lincents very existence is a weakness to all of reality. She is almost as bad as Eogo, I hate Lincent, I just hate her, she needs to die, just get her out my head please. I want to forget about Lincent, get me out of here, she needs to be gone, please, I'm begging you, erase my memories of her, do something please! I don't love her, she's trash! It was a mistake to come to this place that is an insult to my life. Please erase any memory I have of Lincent Kairi Moore, I don't need these freaken feelings, being repulsive is a craving for what must be done, for example watch this." Said Zeth, sounding angry and hateful at first. He slowly, was sounding more sad than angry, it was like as if he was conflicted with what he was saying, and Pakpao didn't make a single response from his statement.

"You see this hag!?! It's a realistic treat of vulgar disrespect in front of your pitiful silence, I'm pissing green with my tally wacker, yah think yah can tolerate this hag, I'd rather become an infant lover than even hold your hag hands. Old hag, maybe your wrinkles should shred your gut wrench body that your demonic soul possesses. Filthy old hag, my hatred for you boils like a vampire feasting on the human of who is a virgin, poo-poo head old hag. You're such a gag, idiotic old hag you don't deserve any supplement of pain relief, which I'm praying to Satan you have pains in your rusty flesh. I refuse to play 'the uncle Tom status' development is just an overrated critic phrase to restrain the hatred within me that gives my mind all kinds of good feelings, and you, old hag and those stupid sidekicks of yours are using development to kill the true hero that saves the only damsel in distress, which is me! And that hero has only one name, and its outrage. So, deal with it old hag before I make you deal with it! May your own self needs be consumed by spiders very slowly, yeah that's what needs to be done, just get it old hag and take it like a deuce." Said Zeth shaking his legs in a vulgar fashion. Pakpao still hasn't said anything yet. "Aren't you mad at me, and why aren't you not ?!" Said a confused Zeth. Both eyes from Zeth and Pakpao were at 'dead center stare' they stared at each other for so long that it was like they were staring into each other's soul.

"Sorrow Zeth sorrow." Said a very sure Pakpao.

"Sorrow? That word is irrelevant to my wellbeing, what makes you think that sorrow has anything to do with me! I'm not sad about anything and never will be" Said Zeth in a bitter tone

"Can you guess why? Said Pakpao.

"Do I have to?" Asked Zeth.

"Please try" Stated Pakpao.

"It's because you think the road, I've been walking led to the nasty verdict of me being this way, right? Yeah that's it isn't it? Well you know what, your right, your absolutely right, that is why I'm like this and let me tell you something, that I could have been much worse than what my current self is, and maybe I should be that current self again." Said Zeth.

"But you won't go back to that level of yours, deep down you hate it, but try to work with it as more of an advisor for the good half of yours, I am correct?" Said Pakpao.

"You're really getting under my skin old hag, that other side of me has always been a guide of light for me, it's what makes me mentally strong, and fights back against any who stand in my way." Said Zeth, who sounded like he was ready to snap.

"That energy of yours, feels so incomplete on both sides, we all know that your energy isn't that of a rightiousful, that's an obvious factor to your spiritual being. However, it's also not entirely for the Insintation either. It doesn't surprise me, to see such a spirit. One that's not too much for either side, tells me that there's a conflict going on that you don't want to admit. You keep trying to act like your full energy is for it but can't bring it down all in all. Even the master Insintation Eogo Ali Tainter was stated to have conflict in his life, but he/she can outweigh the good energy with the bad by a long slide. A lot of Insintations do, which would mean that evil completely shrouds the good into such a small amount that it is powerless against it. For you, that's not the case, or at the very least, not to that degree of shroud, if we're going to be completely honest with each other. If this was going to be estimated, I'd say your good energy takes forty five percent of your soul and evil energy is fifty five percent. No matter how much you deny it, the fact that the good energy has not completely been overwhelmed by the evil energy should not only acknowledge us, but what your being conflicted and torn between. And to you specifically as well, I've got idea as to what it is." Said Pakpao, who at first sounded a bit normal, but then she was getting a little excited with the last half of her worded paragraph.

"Sure, you do" Zeth says sarcastically with a hateful look and tone.

"Eogo Ali Tainter and the Drastics, are you and your cousins Sams family." Said Pakpao while stairing at Zeth with concern in her eyes.

"Oh them" Said a disgusted Zeth who is not looking forward to what Pakpao is about to say.

"Everyone knows what they are like, how they serve for Eogo Ali Tainter, and how they've done so many horrible and sinister things. I could go on about them for an entire year, but that would kind of be off topic with what I'm trying to say, which is how they have affected you." Said Pakpao.

"You can bring the whole bunch, just don't claim uncle Nortric is bad, okay?" Said Zeth.

"Why not Nortric? Have you even heard what he has done to his son Sam? The kind of procedures that he had to go through? How even at the age of being in the womb, Nortric and the judgmisspast experimented on Sam to see that everything is an inevitable perversion. this was all a result of becoming the created monster that Nortric and the Insintation intended. One of the worse things about it, is, we don't even know who the mother is. Zeth, if he did any twisted thing to you, we ca-" ....

"You shut your freaken beak about my uncle, he's a changed man, and went through Hell to protect me, don't you ever talk bad about him again." Rudely interrupted, the outraged Zeth.

"Did he ever tell you that I was his wife?" Asked Pakpao who was trying to keep her emotions in check. Zeth gave the face of complete surprise, with his body trembling for a moment. Nortric did not tell him about this, he might have hinted it, but he never told Zeth about it.

"Nortric would never keep secrets from me, he went to a battle and he fought to the death for my life. There's no way this can be true, I don't believe you, it's all lies, now go away you varmin bird, and never encounter with me again!" shouted a suspicious looking Zeth.

Quickly, Pakpao transformed into a long white-haired woman with white skin, red eyes, cat ears, pink nose and a mouse tail, she was very skinny. Zeth looked even more surprised at what he was seeing. Remembering this womans image on paintings that Nortric used to do. There were some exceptions of others doing it of course, however he never expected this person to be real, and was very curious for more information of who this person was.

"Have you wondered why he never told you about his ex-wife Cressida Drastic? How he manipulated me into thinking that I was the love of his life, when he was cheating in front of me with a red cloaked person that hardly ever reveals her face, and I for the many, have never seen that person's face." Explains Pakpao.

"You were most likely someone of whom, was very abusive to Nortric. I don't blame him. because who would want to remember you anyway, and your still an old hag." Said Zeth while trying to be antagonizing.

"Whatever that man did to make you think he's a nice guy, must be a serious mental affect that you've experienced in your first five years of your life, and I bet Lincent and Sam five coins by that being true." Said a strangely excited Pakpao.

"Nortric promised that I would complete my bloodthirsty revenge on Eogo, who ruined me. The only way to beat evil is to use evil, good is for chickens on the road, while evil is the only true good in the world, and I shall use it like a sword to slay Eogo, and evil will help me accomplish this." Zeth confirms his argument.

"This is an important reason why Zeth, we want you to be the right guy against Eogo, by not having the nature of evil inside. It isn't like those same old stories, where you have no mercy and kill them out of revenge, those are hateful moments. You see what I'm talking about? It's about every time you think, that is what defines your heart." Said Pakpao.

"Nope, just being a bad guy, is enough to rule over sin, now get me out of here, I don't want to ever be at this stupid place again." Said a bitter anxious Zeth

"Okay Zeth, I will set you free, but I have two questions to ask" Said Pakpao.

"Spill em!" Said Zeth, saying it fast with a rude tone "Were you enraged when you found out that Lincent being in a relationship with man that it is not yourself?" questioned Pakpao staring at Zeth like a college teacher making a clarification to a student.

"Na..no! No! There's No way that I'm feeling any jealousy for Sabitchion, She's a loser! A hypocritical sex craving machine! She's. She's... She's just a bad girl!" Proclaims Zeth with his cheeks blushing, and body struggling to not shake over Pakpaos question.

"This an interesting reaction I'm getting, not only is Zeth losing it with my question about Lincent and Sebastian, but after Lincent caught him, and before they were in the barbershop. Zeths energy reminded somewhat natural and then turned darker and darker by them going to the barbershop. Did something about him finding out about David make him try to change his feelings for Lincent? I see Zeth also seemed conflicted with him begging for me to erase his memories of Lincent, this maybe a clue to why Zeth's so mad today, he's afraid that being with Lincent is now impossible, and is upset about it." Remarks Pakpao to herself.

"Okay I answered your question, now get me out of here!" Said Zeth acting like a child.

"Have you forgotten that I said there will be two questions, not one!" Said Pakpao.

"I don't care old hag, your questions hurt my feelings, now get me out!" Zeth repeats while behaving more childish.

"Hurt your feelings?" Asked Pakpao, who laughed after saying her recent words

"Get me out!" Yells Zeth, raising and shaking his arms in anger "Nope" Said Pakpao.

"Pretty please?" Asked a polite Zeth in a soft tone. He was begging on his knees to Pakpao.

"Not until you answer my second question" Returns Pakpao.

"Screw your old hag! screw you! I was trying to be a good brown noser for yah, but I guess that's not grand enough for you nasty tormentors such as yourself, so I'm going to be an obnoxious crazed meth addict that will annoy you to death, get unsteady for the unready." Zeth says with a twitched expression on his face with his hands looking like they were ready for a western gunfight.

"I'm annoying, I'm annoying, i'm oh to Hades with it, what's the second question old hag?" Zeth was changing tone into an exhausted manner. "Do you think you'll be living a happy life with a sinful lifestyle of perversion, or is something deep down inside you that's yearning for the true defeat of sin?" Pakpao said in a very suspicious tone.

Zeths eyes opened wide with his mouth chattering a little in fear, and he wasn't sure what to say about the matter. Pakpao just staired at Zeth, with patience, and waited for what he was going to say.

"I'm not sure" Said Zeth in a normal tone.

Pakpao looked a bit surprised over Zeths answer, she did not expect him to say that, especially in a non-angry tone. Everything was back to normal, Pakpaos appearance returned to redbird form. Not one second or minute has passed in reality, with Zeth looking bitter.

"Before I go, there's something that needs to be clarified." Said a serious Zeth.

"And what is that?" Said Pakpao.

"She'll never see me as someone like that. Not with these past incidents and memories. If Lincent wants to see the good in me, then take away my memories Pakpao. I want a restart of me living in this world with better memories coming in the future!. I know you can do it, a lot of people in this town and outside of it have said you've done it before. I can develop through this, please Pakpao get rid of it so that the evil created by Eogo can be gone from my spirit. I need this gone, please." Said Zeth.

Lincent looked shocked at what Zeth was saying. Sam didn't know the facial expressions, except confusion, and Quinn looked weirded out by all of this. Pakpao however was sad over what Zeth was telling her, she knew that Drastic born children took unimaginable amount of abuse and manipulation in their childhood, and knew that Zeth who really was, a mentally broken person, who lived a life of unforgettable sorrow. Every day Zeth and Sam were plagued by their works on them and might never forget what they have done them. Lincent walked over to Zeth with tears coming down her cheeks. Zeth and Lincent stared at each other with both their heartbeats beating heavily at the intensity of them looking directly into each other's eyes.

"I should slap you for this" Exclaimed Lincent, who sounded like she was ready to bail out crying.

"As long as I have these memories, then evil will always play me, like a kid's toy, and If Pakpao won't get rid of it, then I'm going." Said Zeth

"We haven't done much work on helping you Zeth. Do you remember me saying that you can do it. Why won't you believe that you can?"

Said Lincent with more tears coming down her cheeks and face looking mentally hurt over what was happening.

"Because that 'me' is tainted by Eogo. This made me too shattered to be a good person" Said Zeth, moving his head closer and only an inch away from Lincents face.

"Zeth, I….." Said Lincent with her voice breaking from struggling to contain her crying.

"Zz Ze ze Zeth, I want to …. you, …. I" Said Lincent breaking down with her emotions, being ready to cry. Zeth, while focused on seeing directly into Lincents face, was feeling like he was about to break down crying but shook a bit, from what he was trying to hide.

"Please Zeth? we can accomplish this, I know we can, you've got to believe me, this is the truth, you don't have to erase your memories to do it, please Zeth, please." Said a teared up Lincent, who was begging for mercy on Zeth to reconsider her offered option.

"If Pakpao won't erase my memories, I'm leaving." Said Zeth.

The heartbeats between the two slowed drastically, with both becoming exhausted over the intensity that flows within this conflict. While Pakpao, Sam and Quinn, were not as overwhelmed by the intensity of the conflict, they too could feel the presence of such emotion expressed by Zeth and Lincent.

"I think Pakpao doesn't want to do it. you know what that's gonna mean, right?" Asked Zeth breathing slower and feeling like he was about to have a heavy heart attack from this. He was getting very sexually stimulated. Lincents mouth was closed, no breathing sounds were coming out of her. Lincent felt like she was having a destroyed dream of defeating inequities within a man's heart. She wanted to help Zeth so bad from overcoming such scars, imbedded in his soul, but he wants to erase those thoughts of previous time that he hates. Zeth doesn't want to learn about how to prevent this from happening. He wants it to be unknown in his thought process, and he wants it to be completely nonexistent to him.

"I think I know what you mean by leaving" Said Lincent while tearing up.

"Do you?" Said Zeth.

"Your planning on committing suicide, aren't you?" After Lincent said that, the cornea of her eyes was red from the tears in her eyes, and she looked like she was about to collapse on the floor.

CHAPTER 6

Insinsanity

In HER ROOM, the walls were painted halfway blue by the top half and black on the bottom, with yellow arrow stickers pointing upwards, but those stickers had smaller gray stickers on them, which pointed downwards. The center of the ceiling showed an ox, not anthropomorphic but an ox nonetheless, however the ox only had the back of its body on the ceiling, with the front in scattered pieces around the floor, except the center.

Other paintings showed the four walls. The wall that had the windows, showed a bird like creature, with a black half body on the left and a white half body on the right. On its chest was a brain with red lines that looked smooth, and blue lines that were zigzagged on the brain.

There were words that were written above the bird, and the words were…. 'Everything is negative'

Kalo managed to keep her emotions in check at the sight of the painting, but she didn't like it, at all. The painting on the wall, that was on the left side of the bird wall was a bat, with three drawings under it, that illustrated a shadowy figure killing a bright figure with a knife. The second, was the bright figure killing the shadowy figure with a knife, and the third drawing was both figures dead with a knife stabbed into their chest. Above the bat were words engraved, 'Unnecessary torment'

On the right side of the bird was a rabbit with sperm, flying in between her legs that were bloody, and what spewed was black leeches.

Above the rabbit were the words 'Wiggle wiggle, poison the weener fimble.'

Kalo was horrified because of the drawing, she knew her father hates that drawing but insisted on keeping it in honor of Eogo Ali Tainter.

The painting on the door was a goat, not anthropomorphic like Eogo, but a goat being crushed by a black rock larger than the goat. And the rock had words written in blood engraved 'Burden'

"These paintings that dad thought was a good idea to make, should have never been allowed. I deeply regret letting him make this art that meant to impress the mind of savages. I'm no savage, and once I do this last mission, it will be over, because I know I'm not going to succeed in using sin against them, even if I defeated Sam, which I highly doubt that I would be able to do. Pakpao would definitely be able to annihilate me." Said Kalo to herself.

Kalo, brought the largest preparation of weapons to wear for her last shot in battling against anyone who stood in Jericos way. With a backpack of ninja darts, poison arrows, a sharp dagger, a shield, smoke bomb, dynamite, a small spear, gasoline, some weird ant creatures and other things. This is what Kalo has at her disposal. Kalo had the face and posture of a soldier, however all of that was a camouflage, to hide her true emotions which is nervousness. like a wet naked Chihuahua, her energy went a bit haywire, and her eyes were about to open wide from all of the stress happening around her. She knew this had to be planned through, and if this plan didn't go well, then the worst would happen.

"Conflicted?" Asked Jerico, while opening the door. "I don't. Think so" Said Kalo who felt nervous about Jerico saying that word.

"You sure?" Jerico asked. He was very curious about Kalos energy.

"Your energy... It's on the consideration of turning against me, isn't it?" Jerico questioned. With his eyes slanted and mouth reaching to a tightened point. Kalo walked back a few steps away from Jerico, and her hands were trembling at the sight of him walking towards her. "Aren't you interested in God ascension Kalo?" Said Jerico, while walking slowly and creepily to Kalo.

"I'm not crazy, and that should be addressed very clearly to everyone, especially my daughters." Said a tensed faced Jerico, getting four and a half feet closer to Kalo. Kalo hasn't felt this much fear in all of her life, she began to sweat slowly as it was dripping from her face, her teeth chattering a bit, and eyes looking like she's been having a fever.

"Di, did, did, I, I, I ever sssay you were cra..crazy?" Stammered a stuttering Kalo.

"Kalo !!" Said a strangely calm Jerico.

Both Jerico and Kalo looked at each other intensely showing a gleam in their eyes, with Jerico looking like a cat praying on a rat, and Kalo giving the expression of a scared two-year-old.

With one last intense stare, Jerico spoke in the most serious voice he had ever spoken to Kalo in before. "Energy always entails the mind."

Meanwhile, at the barbershop, with Zeth, Sam. Lincent, and Quinn.

Zeth gave a suspicious appearance from his face, and Lincent looked like she was having the most emotional bad day of her life.

"Is that what you think I'm going to do? Because my plans are about leaving, that's all." Said Zeth.

"Zeth, your energy signifies your depression. How the bright struggles and flickers like a candle light. That's how suicidal people react, feeling like good isn't worth living for anymore. And, I know you don't want that feeling carried any further in your life. But there can be other ways to beat this, please allow me to be your helper in defeating these taints on your soul, I know we've got this, we do Zeth, we do!" Said a sad Lincent.

Lincent grabbed a hold of Zeth tightly, she cried on his chest, and made sure he wouldn't escape from her grasp.

"You weirdo, get off of me, or I'll sue you for sexual harassment!" Said an angry Zeth. "No, I won't let you, you're not going to die, and I'll make sure of it!" Said Lincent, while holding, and looking up at Zeth with a persistent expression on her face. Lincent grabbed a hold of Zeth tightly, cried on his chest, and made sure he wouldn't escape from her grasp.

"You weirdo, get off of me, or I'll sue you for sexual harassment!"

Said an angry Zeth.

"No, I won't let you, your going to die, and I'll make sure of it!"

Said Lincent, while holding and looking up at Zeth with a persistent expression on her face.

"Get off!" Zeth cried while trying to break free from Lincent.

"No" Replied Lincent, who was having no trouble holding Zeth.

Suddenly, the barbershop door opened, which showed a female child monkey, with red marks on her cheeks, light brown fur, red tee shirt and black pants. Her name is Rehema.

"A bird baby is here, it's here!" Said Rehema pointing both her fingers outside.

"Oh no" Said Pakpao, with eyes opened wide.

"We are going to die!" Said a terrified Quinn.

"I can handle this, i'm strong enough to beat it, there's no need to worry guys, this will be done in no time." Sam spoke with confidence.

"Your still not strong enough to fight a baby and this one that survived a blast that could blow up a large mountain is one of the lesser bird babies. This is gonna need to be destroyed by everyone's energy in this town, and I'm not even sure that will work either." Said Pakpao.

"Can we weaken it?" Asked Sam.

"Lesser bird babies do have tubes that help boost their strength, though it would be difficult to beat them because even without the tubes their very strong." Pakpao informed them.

"Then let's go rip those tubes off!" Exclaimed Sam.

"We don't have much time, we've got to do this now, I just have one question before we do." Said Pakpao.

"What's the question?" Asked Sam.

"Have you practiced well in being proficient at dodging?" Pakpao asks. "Just recently, though I'm not sure If I'm a master yet, but I'll do my best." Said Sam.

"Your gonna need to be at least a master level already. This thing is very skilled with its accuracy. Even the people who could withstand large mountain force attacks, have been badly damaged when the arms with the lesser bird babies' hits. You're going to need to take its strength and duration tubes first, if your gonna attack it head on." Said Pakpao.

"Me and David were working on something that might could help defend Sam's wrist." Said Quinn.

"Then you guys, need to get to work on it right away. Sam and i will be outside to gather energy from the people that are aiding Sam in battle by removing the tubes from the bird baby" Said Pakpao.

"Me and Zeth are going to work with David and Quinn, trust me, Pakpao we're gonna get this done pronto!" Said Lincent while grabbing a hold of Zeth.

"I'm not doing anything with you, I said this for the millionth time, I'm leaving and that's final." Said Zeth.

"Lincent, I suggest you get to working with David, Zeth just won't be cooperative, now let's go Sam before the Bird Babu destroys the whole town." Shouted Pakpao, while running out the door.

"Agreed" Said Sam, joining the run with Pakpao.

"We need your help Zeth, please don't leave us!" Said Lincent still holding on to Zeth.

"I would be appreciative if he did leave" Said Quinn.

Lincent gave a mean stare at Quinn, letting the anthropomorphic zebra know how much she's pissed off with her.

"Um, I'll be checking too. Um, working with David on the mechanics." Said a scared Quinn, running to where David was.

Lincent looked at Zeth like a puppy giving a sad face, and Zeth looked down at Lincent with a bitter and mean look on his face. That slowly changed into a sad face which stirred up excitement on Lincents body, knowing that Zeth, isn't who he's trying to make himself out to be.

"She's right about me, I need to to go, this place is not meant for scum like me, I'm sorry but I've got to go." Said a calm but sad Zeth.

Slowly Lincent let go of Zeth, and they both looked at each other's eyes for a moment or two, and Zeth walked out of the door, not looking back. As Lincent saw Zeth leaving, she had to think on helping David with his work on defeating the bird baby, and she needed to be focused on the situation that is at hand.

"Come" Said Quinn, in a strangely soft, calm voice.

"Don't worry Quinn, I'm coming." Said Lincent, as she turned around to see Quinn. But she wasn't there.

"Quinn?" Lincent questioned, looking confused at hearing Quinns voice. She sounded like she was right behind her, but she wasn't, which Lincent found to be odd. As Lincent was walking down the stairs of the barbershop, she was feeling very shaken over this. Hearing no dialogue between Quinn and David, was what she found to be very freaky and was curious into knowing why.

"Quinn!?!? Hello? Can you hear me!?!" Said Lincent, while walking down the stairs, and feeling like she was about to erupt in a panic.

Lincent managed her way down the hallway, she saw Quinn by the furthest distance, which is about twenty feet away from her.

"Are, you, okay Quinn?" Asked Lincent who had a bit of a disturbed look on her face. Quinn, at least from what Lincent can remember, has never behaved like this, and was shaking a little by Quinns current presence. With slower walking speed, Lincent walked towards Quinn, and a possessed face was shown from Quinn, this was raising the tension of Lincents fears for Davids safety up to a maximum. Lincents eyes opened so wide, that the eyes looked as if they were going to be stretched out like a cartoon character. Lincents mouth was closed with a slight chatter, and when she was about to be a foot closer to Quinn, a large red reptile hand dragged Quinn into the room that was behind her. Lincent ran as fast as she could to get into the room, however no one was there, it was all dark.

"Quinn! David! Where are you!?" Called out Lincent.

Suddenly! Electricity sparked from two wires a distance of three feet. In between the wires the electricity formed an image. Lincent walked to it, and what she saw was horrific. In the basement, was either a pre-teen or early teen cat rat, with dark hair, pink sunglasses, brown pants, green shirt, pink nose, rat ears, rat whiskers, a mouse tail, and skin as white as paint. This is Carl Drastic, who has Kalo naked and strapped on a hot steaming pipe.

Kalo screamed in a high pitch! The pain of the hot pipe was arguably the closest thing to burning in Hell.

"Thank your father for allowing me to seize your own gold. That is a good peaceful feeling, and I'm just loving, playing with the body and soul, with even more tools of stealing energy at my disposal." Said Carl

"Even thinking of using members of the judgmisspast is horrid, but this needs to be done. My daughter cannot live a life of being beneath the one that should be executed. I'm sorry Kalo please forgive me." Said Jerico with sadness shown on his face.

"I love how you don't realize, that you're a sick lunatic, crazy like us. how you let Eogo advise your own path, into a shred of spiritual gold from your kids. Oh, how it stimulates my sexual hormones. If only the kids at your magic kingdom, would have fun with a happy talking 'pedo-grab-in-hold'. The long and short finger clash. How such a child with spiritual gold, loses that gold to a pot bearded man who unzips his pants right behind them, spiritual gold is so-......" Carl couldn't finish his sentence, while interrupting in anger. "Don't you ever say i'm one of you. I've kissed your boss's pedo ass for too long. Paying such a price with Eogo, and this daughter problem is as far as I'm going to be anywhere near you guys, I'm not even interested in getting a bird baby either." Kalos back was melting from the hot pipe, Carl cut her breast in two, and put steampunk beetles in there.

Carl chuckled as he was drilling his fingers into Kalos knees, and something burst out of Carls left leg. It was a gooey fat partially skeletal cat that was slithering around Kalos waist and the pipe.

Kalo's screams echoed outside of the basement and Carl just imitated everything she was doing. Chainsaw sounds were heard all around them, and Carls head began to shake and twitch like a broken electronic toy.

"Maah, mmaahh laalffva! Now you're the scoundrel with watashi!" Sung Carl while taking his clothes off.

"The spiritual gold, gold, gooollld!" Sung Carl, who bent his body in a scissor shape form and began to slowly cut Kalos skin.

"Workout your gold then! yyyooouurrrr mmmaaoolld!"

Sung Carl whose neck rose up in a snake like manner, and slammed through Kalos left eyeball, spitting oil on her face. "Maah, mmmaaahh laalffca, now you're the scoundrel with watashi, the spiritual gold, gold, gaaooold, without your gold then yourrr mmmmmmaaoold that is old!" Sung Carl spinning his head around in Kalos skull.

Crocodiles with bird heads whose skin is inside out arrived from a duplicated head from Carl that partially transformed into tornadoes that smack poop and sewage waste on Kalo.

The poop and sewage waste rolled all over her body and stretched out ten feet long. The poop and sewage transformed into mechanical steampunk dogs that carved words on Kalo's belly which spelled 'useless white squirt from Jerico' The partial tornadoes shot out seeds into Kalos belly button, and her belly was bubbling black and orange, with acne spewing out. Cyborg steampunk's mechanical like worms emerged from her belly button, that aligned themselves together spelling 'Mommy' The cyborg steampunk worm was turning glowing red, which engraved the words on her belly and they also heated up so high that blue flame was coming from them.

"Can me have da fun?" Said Iaintyobuddy who was standing right behind Kalo.

"Her gold shall be taken away even more!" Carl puts his word in.

Iaintyobuddy gave a sadistic laugh. He walked in front of Kalo and when he was in front of her, he was already naked. Kalo was still screaming in horrendous pain at what was happening to her, and Carl's pupils went up so high, that only his cornea was showing.

"Everything that the judgmisspast wanted, coming smoothly well with Eogos plans, isn't that correct Carl?"

Muttered Iaintyobuddy who was sexually rubbing his hands on Kalos melted hips. Iaintyobuddy rubbed his face on Kalos torn breast, started to suck the blood from her, and orally blew new blood into her, that gave her cancer. The blood contained many kinds of viruses, cancer, and lupus. When Kalo peed, the bladder was not only green, but the steaming blood was red.

"The gold stolen in the name of thirty-three, thirty-three, thirty-three." Sung Carl and Iaintyobuddy while chewing her melted butt cheeks. Slowly Iaintyobuddy was ripping Kalos legs apart from her body and when the skin was tearing Carl spat at it, as a form of mockery to Kalo. When the bone began to crack, the giant anthropomorphic hippopotamus took pieces of the bone off from her and swallowed the pieces. As the legs fully came off, Kalo's screaming was weakening, and Carl knew she was dying from the damages on her body. Carl injected different types of organisms to keep her alive, just so he could do more sadistic things to her. Iaintyobuddy's skin temporally turned pale right before it turned back to normal, he vomited sperm, poop, urine, placentas, gasoline, giant cell organisms, blood from periods, old monkey milk, of shark teeth, a pool of month old ketchup, old french fries with mustard on them, a pool of new mustard, twenty feet tall intestines that slithers around like a snake, ashes, swords, rubys, dead baby dragons, a dead baby bird, and other things.

Then, what Iaintyobuddy vomited morphed into a rainbow like a 6'5" green anthropomorphic lizard that exploded into pieces right onto Kalo, which destroyed her skin.

While Carl, was somewhat reviving Kalos body with needle injections, this was intentionally made to be painful and caused Kalo to scream the loudest she possibly could. As she was losing her skin.

Carl sliced her right hand, clean off from her arm, and threw the hand right at Iaintyobuddys nose, which he sucked in with his left nostril. He injected some more needles into her arms, which grew multiple hands on her right arm. They were sliced off by Carl as he threw those arms at Iaintyobuddy, who eats the arms with his buttcheeks.

"I ffa, ffffaaa, ffffaaeeeelll herpi, pieces Innnnnnnnaaaa me!" Said a deep voiced Iaintyobuddy while his tongue was licking his eyeballs. "Ssssssaaaarrrgory!" Said a feminine voiced Carl who was checking his sparkled purse for tools to use for Kalos surgery.

Jerico teared up at the sight of his daughter being tortured by Carl and Iaintyobuddy. However, despite the fact that he was tearing up over this, both Carl and even Iaintyobuddy knew he was sick in the head for allowing them to do this to her. Carl, Iaintyobuddy and Jerico are out of their minds, with the only difference being that Carl and Iaintyobuddy know they are crazy but Jerico thinks this is a necessary discipline.

He believes that Kalo has been conflicted for far too long. Finally, he decides to do something he never thought he could do. that allowed Carl to statistically and sadistically torture her, in the worst way possible.

Due to the needle injections on Kalos melted body, her screams sounded more demonic and made hissing snake sounds. Her only eye blackened with a glowing red snake pupil. Something was forming, with Kalo turning into gooy black bubbles.

"I shall call you Faveriod" Said Carl. After the footage ended, Lincent saw a pool of blood drooling down on the electric field in front of Lincent. What she saw was Kalos full transformation into Faveriod. Meanwhile Kalo was chewing the flesh off Quinn.

Kalo with the orange glowing reptile eyes, grew a new body, with shadowy red skin, sabertooth claws, long bird legs, her head formed into a crocodile's head, with four-foot-long horns on her neck, and she stood over ten feet tall.

Lincent screamed!! in terror of the sight of what had happened to Kalo and there was an electric collar on Faveriod Kalos chest and out of it came the voice of Kalo saying. "The rabbit bastard caught with the line-sex-dog, and then Zeth!"

Meanwhile with Sam and Pakpao

While looking at the bird baby, both Pakpao and Sam were outside and saw the bird baby walking and limping to the town. Its appearance had a gray bird like features, with muscular green reptile arms, eagle wings, owl head, anthropomorphic eagle legs, black pants, with tubes on its back. The first tube being "speed/accurate". The second, "near infinite stamina". The third the "duration", and fourth the "strength."

"Any news on Quinn and David getting the mechanics for your defence?" Questioned Pakpao.

"Unfortunately, nothing" Said a disappointed Sam.

"Well fooy, I was hoping they would have something ready in time, but we need to take this thing down now." Said Pakpao.

"Yes indeed" Said Sam'

"But before we get started, there's something else you need to know about the bird baby." Said Pakpao.

"Tell me" Said Sam. "what If the bird baby detonates itself, a countless number of people will die? It's going to do that? I'm going to need to use my secret stored energy. I've been storing this up for a while." Said Pakpao

"What kind of energy?" Questioned Sam.

"This kind of energy that will send the bird baby to another dimension, will need to be used well, because our options are running out."

"That sounds like a good backup plan, now let's gather the energy to defeat the bird baby." Said Sam.

Five minutes later, with Pakpao and the mayor convincing everyone to give Sam enough multiplication of power to stand a chance against the bird baby. As the bird baby got into town, Sam with the bright gathered energy, managed to sneak up behind the bird baby, and remove two of the tubes which was 'strength' and 'duration' but failed to get the others because the bird baby reacted fast enough to attack Sam before he could do his task.

The punch was a hit to the left side of Sams cheek, causing him to bleed and almost had his cheekbone broken on impact. With the number of punches being over 50,000 punches per microsecond, the bird baby kept hitting Sam like as he was a teddy bear being torn up by an actual bear. Sam couldn't defend himself that well, against any of the punches that were delivered by the bird baby. If the bird baby had its strength, that would have greatly helped multiply the force of its speed. Sam would have been punched into pieces, not to mention that this is what the bird baby is capable of in a weaken state from the explosion that it withstood.

Sam kicked the bird baby's leg, causing it to almost fall, this gave Sam the advantage to take away the speed/accuracy tube from the bird baby, which Sam did, and he kept hitting the bird baby continuously with his fist, legs, and knees.

The bird baby managed to kick Sam on the hip, and punched for a long while on his face, until Sam fortunately grabbed both of its fists, while he jumped, and knee kicked the bird baby on the beak. In a barbaric fashion of a moment, both Sam and the bird baby laid punches on each other's faces. Moving the punches to the hips for a moment, and pretty much all over the front of their bodies, but eventually Sam was beginning to do more and more contacts on the bird baby, which made Sam excited.

"This place will never be conquered or be destroyed by the likes of you, now get ready to be trashed!" Yelled Sam while overwhelming the bird baby.

Sam, in a figure of speech, was on fire punching, kicking and beating the bird baby until Sam's speed and strength oddly decreased, which gave the bird baby the opportunity to smack Sam on his face and continuously kept hitting him. The bird baby grabbed Sam's legs and threw the legs to a house, which caused the house to be destroyed on impact. The bird baby jumped like a frog to Sam and punched his arms so much that it resulted to injury. In distress Sam attempted to punch the bird baby away from him, but the bird baby grabbed ahold of his right arm, spun around like a tornado and threw him to another house, which was also destroyed on impact. Again, the bird baby jumped like a frog to reach to Sam and kept on punching him all over his body.

"What in the world is happening? When Sam was able to remove the tubes, he had a lot of energy from everyone in town, now the energy is diminishing and getting weaker by the second! The only way this could happen, is if (A) their being killed off, (B), their energy is stolen, or "C."……

Shortly after Pakpao said the letter C, her eyes opened wide and said. "Oh no!!!!" Quickly Pakpao went into spirit form, to see what was going on, and saw most of the people's energy turning dark.

"So, letter C does have a sinister play here doesn't it?" Said Pakpao whos face tightened over what was happening. "Guess I've got some work to do" Said Pakpao using her energy on the people. However, when she did this, Jerico and Faveriod Kalo used their energies on the people to counterfeit Pakpaos doing.

"These people will embrace 'god ascension' or die Pakpao" using Said Jerico while his energy on the people.

"That monster, you haven't done anything like this before in a while! Don't tell me you've allowed the Judgmisspast and Carl to make a monster for you?" Said Pakpao, looking tensed while using her energy on the people.

"Kalo was in conflict for far too long. Someone had to fix her, so I brought Carl to do the job. Gosh darn it! she's become a bad Satanist again, and now it's time for these people to be born again too." Said Jerico using his dark energy as a goal to corrupt the people's minds into 'god ascension'.

"You really are a savage" Said a disgusted Pakpao pushing forth more energy on the people.

Meanwhile with Lincent.

Lincent, was in a rusty cage made by Carl Drastic. She saw David in the distance, not locked up, but he was bawling tears at the sight of Faveriod Kalo who was remaining in spirit form, as a dark spiritual warrior, going to battle with Jerico.

"David!" Alerts Lincent, losing a bit of self-control of her emotions over what was happening.

"Mommy whaaaa …. what's happening!?!" Cries out David while bawling in an upset manner.

"David look at me. Everything's going to be alright, we'll get out of this, I promise!" Said Lincent, while grabbing onto the bars.

"There's nothing you can do about what I have in store. This little boy will love what he has left in this, and will view it with hatred for this world, just like my boss!" Said Carl, with the electric imagery, showing him give his speech. "What is it with you? taking peoples happiness for living life, in this world? Especially for a child here. Why do you like seeing that why?" Cries out Lincent who was furious over the position Carl was putting David through. "It's just what me, and my greatest teacher, the Judgmisspast, likes to do." Said Carl smiling like a feme nit homosexual.

"I don't buy it. You must have had a bad childhood, like Sam and Zeth, and the same can be said, for almost any Drastic born that was ruled by Eogo Ali Tainter." Said Lincent.

"Sure, whatever short cakes, now let's wait for the real cookie monster, who will arrive any time now. Bringing evil energy of the judgmisspast minions." Said Carl.

"What cookie monster?" Questioned Lincent.

Carl gave a sadistic smile infront of Lincent and laughed like a madman in a padded cell.

Meanwhile with Zeth.

While walking almost a mile from the town, Zeth thought about the worth of staying or leaving. On one side, staying might be beneficial for him to rebuild himself from thinking sin is good to conquering it. However, he's in question about whether this will work or not. So far, his thinking about it, does not, outweigh him considering it to work. Then there's the leaving concept that brings forth uncertainty alone in a void, dealing with 'how to take down enemies himself'. All three, and maybe more of these possibilities, gave hesitation in Zeths mind. He wants to believe that he can do it all himself, but both the questioning of uncertainty and him being alone in all of this, could make him nothing, with a bitter hateful way of living. Just viewing his life as a ruthless burnt-out one-man army against the forces of evil. Zeth, could imagine himself struggling his way through, slaying his enemies, and overcoming the weight of sin into his own way and no one else. It's a lot like trying to apply a badass vibe to someone's behavior, which is a drive that Zeth wouldn't mind taking once and a while. It would be like a drink with sugar, it may not be healthy but at least it's a good taste for a few drinks occasionally. What's motivating him to a high degree to do this, is that he wants to be above any attachments, that he could lose. Zeth doesn't want to have anything to do with that anymore, it's a pain that shatters him, like a painting painted years and years ago, being destroyed. Zeth wants to get rid of that, but at the same time, he feels that sense, that calling to try it, for at least one more time.

Zeths tightened skin turns beet red. He walks away from that calling. The thoughts amplified in his mind. It almost made him have a mental breakdown from this decision. He looked back at the town, wondering about himself.

"The bird baby, Lincent, David, Sam and everyone else. Should I save them or go the 'to Hell with them route'? Asked Zeth to himself.

Zeth looked at the mountains, with his face shaking a bit from the decision he was having trouble choosing from. If he goes back, then there might be a chance for him to save the people who might want to be his friends, especially Lincent. Lincent was determined to help him.

But if he continues any further away from the town, then it would be too late. Lincent and everyone else would either be killed or serve for Jericos goal for god ascension. Zeths thoughts amplified greatly, of thoughts that would happen to them, which made his face redder and more tightened.

He couldn't handle the thoughts and says. "Screw it!"

"See the hurt vessels David? do you see it? I bet it's shrieking your nerves, with the loud screams that exclaim the horrors that are my wonders. Panic from it, David, Panic!" Exclaimed Carl, while showing tortured naked people being torn apart from their bodies by Iaintyobuddy. David was crying and yelling, he was upset at what Carl was trying to show him.

"Stop traumatizing my son you sicko!" Yelled Lincent.

"Hear them being hurt David? listen to the voices that scar you mentally!" Yelled Carl. The yelling in agony and pain was getting louder, with more people being tossed to Iaintyobuddy by deformed creatures. When they were brought to Iaintyobuddy, they were being torn to pieces.

"YYEEEAAAAZZZZ, hahahahahha, theerrrrrrnaaa gra, gra, gratah for me Cracken!" Yelled Iaintyobuddy, while destroying and eating the bodies of the people.

For a while, the people were screaming in agony at what Iaintyobuddy was doing to them, until Carl used a machine that contained needles that injected black goo with red dots in them. This made the tortured people get pleasure from what Iaintyobuddy was doing to them. Meanwhile Iaintyobuddy was making sexual sounds while removing their body parts.

"Stop what you're doing, i'm here to save the day!" Said Zeth while holding a two-and-a-half-foot wooden sword.

"Zeth!" Cried out Lincent in excitement

"Zzeeaath!" Yelled Carl, with eyes opened wide, and mouth smiling.

"Butthole!" David screams with an angry face.

"David, don't say those bad words!" Said Lincent.

Carl laughed and popped his knuckles that for some reason caused Faveriod Kalo to spit out an electronic box with crab legs that walked towards Zeth.

"I'm gonna die!" Said Zeth, with body shaking in a poor defensive posture.

"Tell yah what Zeth, if you withstand the suppressed 'weaker than a child hits' from this creation of mine, then I won't lay a finger on these two-precious people." Said Carl.

"Oh please, like this thing can beat me, just you wait Carl, when I slay this beast, your next to be slain." Zeth was shaking in fear as the machine arrived to Zeth, it broke his wooden sword with a rotten a green hand popping out. "You better do it, or you know God knows what will be of Lincent and David." Said Carl. Zeth looked at both Lincent and David, with a nervous expression on his face.

"I believe in you Zeth!" Lincent tells Zeth.

Zeth with a serious but nervous stare at Lincent, took a deep breath at what he was about to do and say.

"I'll do it" Said Zeth.

Zeth with eyes focused down at the machine, felt extremely unprepared for what it had in store for him.

"Keep your arms behind your back please. This is something that will be adored and seen by the Judgmisspast children. So, do it" Explains Carl.

Zeth put his hands behind his back. He felt even more afraid of the machine box. And knew that this was going to hurt him a lot.

"Start up to 25% of a two old boys smack attack potency." Orders Carl, smiling like as if he just got married.

Out of the box, came the green hand, and it smacked Zeths face on the exact level of attack potency that Carl told it to do. Zeth clenched his teeth at what the green hand did to him, because it felt like someone was drilling through his cheeks with tigers' claws.

"Now for 35% of a five-year-old boys punch on the belly!" Carl orders again, looking like a football fan seeing his team heading towards the goal. When the green hand did that, Zeths face turned red, and screamed out loud. In pain as he was currently feeling....

the blow. Zeth was in so much pain that tears were coming down from his eyes, and he nearly collapses onto the floor.

"Zeth, you are as pathetic as you were before, with hardly any physical improvements seen in the slightest. You can't even handle a kid punch that well. I shouldn't be ranting about this, I should be laughing until my satisfaction has approached the end of reality, which I'll do right now." After Carl proclaimed his sentence, he laughed like someone watching their favorite comedian telling their best joke, and almost im- mediately switched in a serious tone of voice saying. "Now do a pre-teen male punch on the belly."

The green hand did just that, which caused Zeth to fall on the ground and vomit on the floor.

"Looks like we have a real F- winner Zeth, oh how your uncle would be so proud, getting the 'not-so-manly' vibe to your own character."

Immediately after Carl said that, he laughed with Zeths response being.

"Screw you!"

Carl gave a childlike smile, he knew this was getting on Zeths nerves, and chose another painful thing to use that would hurt Zeth, even worse than the hits from the green hand.

"I've got images, darn good images, of something you don't want to ever see again, because of the 'I-love-nightmare' images that Eogo threw you into. Yes Zeth, those images." Carl claims. As he smiled like someone hiding a big secret for a surprise.

"Please, don't tell me what I think it is" Said Zeth who almost immediately changed from feeling like he was in serious pain, to fear of his secrets being shown in public.

"These images are one of your biggest shocking experiences"

Exclaimed a sinister faced Carl.

CHAPTER 7

Back To Now

ZETH SCREAMED IN fear at what Carl was about to show. It gave Carl pleasure from seeing Zeth's mental breakdown.

"David! cover your eyes!" Yelled Lincent.

As David was covering his eyes, Carl pointed at him and said. "Open them or burn! David did just that, with tears coming down from his eyes.

Carl ran his tongue over his own lips very sensual like. Lincent was so mad at what was happening, that she wanted to rip out Carls eye sockets and ring his neck. With the images being shown, Lincents face appeared frozen, from what she was seeing as David passes out because of the overwhelming stress on him. The images showed Zeth as a child, torturing and destroying anthropomorphic people. He was also using mental abuse on them. He used energy of ruining people's sanity by the help of other wicked people joining in doing this.

He poured gasoline and burned children of all ages in front of the parents, and then by using robotic arms, he ripped their arms and legs off. He strangled a six-year-old to death by telling Iaintyobuddy what to do, and he also told the giant hippopotamus to do unspeakable crimes that were against women's will. Iaintyobuddy did this in front of the husbands and children of the women.

Zeth told Iaintyobuddy to send those families into a place that would destroy their minds. They would always suffer. Zeth did a lot of horrible things to the people, but from the images being shown, he never looked sadistically happy from doing this to them. Like as if he was to do it.

"Isn't that a lame 'wimp out' over what Eogo was going to put you back into? The world of un-resisting, and every Drastic knows why! That world is a black foot that walks like a spider in your skin. You just couldn't take it, the amplifications poured down in Zeth's skull like a cup. I do believe those images of amplifications on why you chose to do those tortures, instead of going back to that, is what rumbles in an earthquake on Zeths lifetime." Exclaimed Carl with his hands held tightened together. Zeth grabbed and pulled his hair in a panic at what Carl was planning to show next.

"No, naoh, no"! Cried a teared up Zeth, shaking on the ground. At this moment, Lincent was seeing Zeth's sorrow, over being reminded of his past, she knew what he did was awful but also knew of the threatening horrors of not doing them, especially when Eogo is involved with it. Knowing that evil amplifications had a part to play with all of this, has put Lincent into thinking how bad Zeth could have been. Could he have been a continuous rapist? A monster fueled with darkness and a urge to make more children of disobedience upon the face of the maker? What did the amplifications do to Zeth? What level of evil did it turn him into?

These questions made Lincent realize at a higher degree, on why Zeth behaves like a jerk, and that Zeth could be a sweet heart in comparison to what he fears to be. This made Lincent concerned over Zeth and was saddened to see him in this state of misery.

"I don't fully understand why you don't embrace your sins Zeth, this is a work of art, why don't you see that? Remember how the amplifications changed your thought process? Why not go back to that? The good ole times, not the era of regretting the doings of sin, be welcomed back into the arms of the Drastic family and become an Insintation!" Exclaimed Carl with a mad happy face, and eyes slanted with joy.

"Never!" Yelled Zeth while still laying on the floor with tears coming out of the eyes.

"You were about that, because you did wimp out. You were not trying to resist those amplifications and chose the cowardly route, face it! By the inspirational quote of Sam, 'evil is inevitable' Exclaimed Carl.

"Not if you can find a way to beat it, which Sam did, and Zeth can do it all." Lincent replies to Carl.

"It was only because Eogo became absent later on, with only rumors on why he/she did that, and I can assure you If Eogo was back, these guys would be nuts again, and you're in a foolish denial of it." Answers Carl.

"He's right I'm a-" Lincent quickly interrupted Zeth trying to finish what he was about to say and says. "Oh, just shut the Hell up Zeth, you seriously need to stop doubting yourself, and take your responsibilities like a man. Not like some whiner who keeps living in the past, that horror is done, now we've got to push forward and take down the evils that seeks, whomever they may devour. That is the Zeth that is needed, and you can do it!" Almost immediately after Lincent said that, Faveriod Kalo jumped up, crashing through the ceilings, with Carl giving the response of. "What thw crap!" A boulder was thrown on the machine box. Who do you think arrived down from the ceiling? It was Pakpao.

"How in the fuzz did you do that!?!!" Yelled a very angry Carl.

"It was as easy as eating a chocolate icing cake." Said Pakpao, looking very proud of herself.

"That's not an answer, tell me!" Yelled an upset Carl.

"Sorry, I don't speak to people, who speak the language called angry brats" Said Pakpao

"Go in a cursed acid serpent, you're an anus breath!" After Carl yelled that out loud, the device that showed him through the imagery blew up, and Pakpao, with just a smack of her feathery hands, destroyed the cage that Lincent was in.

"How did you do it Pakpao?" Questioned Lincent.

"Let's just say, Carl isn't really that good in keeping his experiments mentally stable in terms of inner conflict, now we better help Sam the best way we can with your mechanics." Said Pakpao.

"What about Jerico, is he dealt with?" Questioned Lincent again.

"At the time I was influencing Kalo, Jerico lost his control over influencing the people. That gave me the advantage, bringing them back to good energy. He was very mad at me doing that" Said Pakpao.

"No doubt about that, but Pakpao, there's something I need to ask you." Said Lincent with a tired yet concerned expression on her face.

"What is he asking?" Asked Pakpao as Lincent pointed at the passed-out David with Pakpao giving the response of. "Oh."

Meanwhile with Sam.

After a countless amount of hits on Sam, he was all beaten up from the fight, even though he's got his energy back. The damage took a toll on his body, that almost made him give up. There on the ruins of a house, was Sam whose appearance was bruised on many parts of his body, and the bird baby ran to him again, ready to deliver an elbow slam to Sam's face. Sam jumped above the bird baby and kicked it on the back. This action Sam did, was the luckiest move he made against the bird baby and doesn't believe he'll get another lucky shot like that again.

Suddenly Pakpao and Lincent arrive with many kinds of weaponry.

"Sam, put this on!" Yelled Pakpao, tossing two blue balls with black x on them, and a button on the center. As Sam caught the balls, the bird baby was ready to fight back, which put Sam in a state, of somewhat panic.

"What does it do!?" Yelled Sam. Completely scared of the object.

"Press the button and defend yourself with it!" Replied Pakpao.

When Sam pressed the button, the ball was glued onto him, and as the bird baby was about to punch him, Sam out of a strange instant reflex, defended against the punches.

"Sam, say glue cage!" Yelled Pakpao

"Glue cage!" Yells sam.

Immediately after Sam said those words, it was at the time when the bird baby's fist punch made a hit to the balls. It swallowed its arms, and it couldn't escape from it.

"Now say release me!" Yelled Pakpao.

"Release me!" Said Sam, and the balls let go of Sam, but held onto the bird baby.

"Now say burn cage!" Yelled Pakpao.

"Burn cage!" Yelled Sam. The balls turned hot steaming red, which was causing the bird baby's arms to slowly melt.

"Now rip it's arms off!" Coached Pakpao.

Carefully not touching the balls, Sam ripped the bird baby's melted arms off, and kept beating it down to the ground, until it was unable to move.

A red light flickered on its chest, and Pakpao's eyes opened wide and says. "Time to use the desperate plan!" Pakpao picked up a small red box out of her pocket, crushed it, and what showed was a vortex of some sort, and Pakpao blasted it to the bird baby, which caused it to disappear." If the bird had not succeeded in self-destruction here, we all would have died, if not, much more of us." Said Pakpao.

"That was some tough papers to read, I'm so glad it was something that David showed me recently otherwise, we would have been overwhelmed by the raw power of the bird baby." Said Lincent.

"Lincent, there's something I need to say to both you, David, and everyone else." Said Zeth.

"Before you do, David must be treated with a lot of love and care now, from what he has witnessed. Can you make the commitment?" Lincent questions.

"I sure need to" Said Zeth.

Lincent looked at Zeth, with a discerning look on her face, letting him know how serious the matter was.

"I will Lincent, I will. It is the least of what I can do, to apologize" Zeth complies. Lincent walked over to Zeth, and when she was right in front of him, she hugged Zeth, with the happiness of a soldier coming home from war. "Thank you" Said a soft toned grateful Lincent.

Meanwhile with Jerico.

In a dark room that was perfectly clean, with a well-made green covered bed, purple carpet, and white walls and ceiling. With the door open,

Jerico appeared with a forced happy face. The kind of face that a husband would portray when his wife comes home after four in the morning.

As Jerico walked to where he was going, he was holding a rose with white feathers keeping the bunch neatly together. The bottom of the feathers was pointy shaped like ox horns. Jerico was right in front of where he was walking towards and did a bow. Jericos eyes looked saddened with his mouth, having trouble to say even a word. While trying to come up with the right words, Jerico took a deep breath with eyes stretched open, but slanted. Jerico says. "Just like your life, hers had to be altered as well, and I was right at the very point of making it permanent. Unfortunately, due to Carl's failure in perfecting such makings, Kalo is now gone, our un-decided warrior of rising above, has abandoned us my sweet. If only I had gotten onto his case for that. Then that rugged bird, would never have pulled the bad she has done! People need god ascension, and this monster that is within me, will do the job, one way or another, it will do it, so help me God. I will swear on myself, and the people who follow me, that I'll soon release Savage and bring forth perfect god ascension with no back stabbers, and no 'one-eighties act.' Etc. This is how it's going to be done my love. I know you may have had difficulty in coming into an agreement with me, however when i grabbed your head and shoved it at the window, what you saw was the 'marvelous future'. That continuous reaching out for law and power, which is beyond any dimension that we can imagine. Eogo had notified me, that Savage is capable in achieving such a feat. Why? Are people so conflicted with my teachings? Can't they get notice here that I am their true Allie !?" Said Jerico, who at first sounded nervous and yet calm, except with the last words he put in his paragraph being. "This is a human need of gaining power, and by my swear, the swear of truth, justice, heroics, righteousness, virtuosity, sanity, and power, 'I Jerico,' will slay the hungry god of power with these words as my signature. Yectua damned, Yectua damned for suppressing god ascension, and may Yectua be damned to Hell!" Cried out Jerico in a savage like state.

1980 11:25 PM

With their speeds rising above picosecond, femtosecond, and yoctosecond, the combative speed of Caprin and the 'bright winged fighter' (BWF for short) was up to a number of combative speed is googleplexian hits per yoctosecond times itself in a yoctosecond for over a thousand years, which was calculated by brilliant people, but even those calculations couldn't reach to the exact number because it broke the measurements. This combative speed is called U.C.S. Caprins sword from the first yoctosecond of its existence was able to surpass a master samurai cutting attack potency by times undecillion and its attack potency keeps increasing by times undecillion of every femtosecond of its existence, and this sword is over trillions of years old. Although its full power is yet uncertain, and likely far higher. BWFs defense was prepared for this with small razor blade shields on his wrist to defend himself against Caprins attacks. What the sword can withstand is almost unbreakable, with only an all-powerful creator being able to destroy it, a Brax-lung sword, an ability Eogo possesses, or technically it is returning to the void, the name of this sword is 'Xifos Gia Midenismo'. An example of how much this sword can withstand has been up to far greater than infinite dimensional attack potency of the Hilbert Spaces. When a being, that had no dimensional limitation couldn't destroy 'Xifos Gia Midenismo' Or a character that can cut through the fabric of reality and can't damage 'Xifos Gia Midenismo.' However, an all 'powerful being' can destroy it. Caprin was so powerful here, that if Zeth fought him against this power, Zeth would have died in one hit very easily, and the reason why Zeth survived Caprin is because Caprin suppressed his power in fighting Zeth, for that in truth Caprin is vastly superior to Zeth Drastic.

Both Caprin and BWF were rivaling each other in speed, and they created huge amounts of duplicates of themselves.

The first duplicates were about the same, with Caprin being able to bring forth the speed and attack potency of 'Xifos Gia Midenismo.'

The second duplicates were BWF sending energy blast on the level of attack potency far greater than what a super nova and gamma ray burst could ever reach, with Caprin just simply punching them away.

The third duplicates were Caprin shrinking a five hundred trillion-mile steel block to more than a thousand times smaller and weaker than a cell in less than a Yoctosecond, and a lot more blocks were sent by BWF towards Caprin.

The fourth duplicates were BWF using an energy attack that made him infinitely faster than Caprin, but the bat, used his own Cordblock which is a lot better than Zeth's, with him equalizing speed, even by beings infinitely faster than him. With Caprins master

Cordblock level 1, he can equalize his faster opponents speed down to his and make himself five point five times faster than his opponent.

Master Cordblock level 2 is equalized speed down to his, by characters who are infinitely faster than infinite speeds times faster than him. He can be two point two five times faster than them. And finally, Master Cordblock level 3 is beyond any infinity that has ever been calculated times his own speed.

Caprin can only use one offensive attack, for every single minute, and cannot move his legs faster than 28 MPH in a 100-meter sprint, and it takes a lot of focus to use this power.

Just to be safe, Caprin used Master Cordblock level 2, and defeated BWFs fourth duplicate.

The fifth duplicate was, him seeing through a lot of the warriors lives in less than a femtosecond by experiencing their lives, he now knows their strengths and weaknesses.

The sixth duplicate was Caprin turning invisible to hide from BWF and surprise attack BWF, however BWF knew where he was and killed Caprins sixth duplicate.

The seventh duplicate was Caprin adapting to breathing underwater, however BWF created a new form of water in the sky that was an ocean above, that slowed down Caprin's capability speed and drowned Caprin's sixth duplicate to death.

The eighth duplicate was Caprin causing fast Alzheimer's on BWF, which caused the eighth duplicate of BWF to forget how to fight, which resulted Caprin being able to easily kill the eighth duplicate of BWF.

The ninth duplicate was Caprin using an ability called Phyoken, which breaks the laws of physics. In this example, if somebody threw a boulder at you, instead of going backwards, you go forwards. Caprin almost used this ability to send BWF towards him, however BWF killed the ninth duplicate of Caprin quickly, so that he wouldn't do it.

The tenth duplicate was Caprin considering using min-duction, which reduces the attack potency of nearly everything, for example when if someone was able to kill some character infinitely more powerful than any hyperversal being, he can reduce their attack potency down to zero dimensional or of a snail. Another example is someone being able to cut through the fabric of reality and Caprin can shrink that level of attack down to zero dimensional or that of a snail. Caprin, almost used this ability, but BWF managed to lay a fatal hit on his chest, which caused the tenth duplicate of Caprin to die.

The eleventh duplicate of Caprin, nearly killed BWF's eleventh duplicate. It was continuously cutting BWFs body far much more than googleplexian pieces, however BWF used an amazing healing factor that regenerates BWF's body on the speed of Caprins combat, which led to this fight being almost without end. It should be noted: that the reason why, BWF was not affected by the poison is because, he became immune to the toxins.

The twelfth duplicate was, Caprin using an ability to effect BWF's nervous system, called Nervdone, and succeeded in doing so, but BWF used a counter act to this, called Antinervdone, which gave him resistance to this, and Caprin used counter Antinervdone which turned off the resistance, this horribly upset BWF, and ripped the twelfth duplicate of Caprins body clean off.

"How does that feel numbnuts?" Questioned an offensive BWF.

With the thirteenth duplicate of Caprin, and with BWF in motion, Caprin used a power that was within 3-dimensional, and in between the power of planetary and universal. Caprin can clone his opponents by their level of duration, attack, potency, speed, strength and abilities, and might can do this with higher dimensional powers but that's yet unknown. Caprin was about to create the clone in less than a yoctosecond, but BWF killed the being processed clone of himself, and killed the thirteenth duplicate of Caprin too.

"Yeah, nice try bro, but that ain't gonna happen, you dirty blood sucker!" Exclaimed a furious BWF.

The fourteenth duplicate of Caprin was kicked in the face by BWF and Caprin used an ability called Ninitythstam, that takes away more than 99.99% of someone's stamina. The energy that shot out of his body looked like black sand, BWF dodged it. As the fourteenth duplicate of BWF was heading towards Caprin to hit him, Caprin used an ability called the backfire hurt. Whenever someone hits Caprin, it hurts, damages or kills them instead. When BWF punched Caprin on the face, it damaged BWFs face, which gave Caprin the advantage to kill the fourteenth duplicate of BWF.

In actuality, the 'back fire hurt' is so effective, that even beings that it has cut through a reality beyond any dimensional concept, and even far beyond that. When Caprin uses the back fire hurt, characters with that level of attack potency are hurt instead.

Another example, is a character with a sword, that cut threw the fabric of any universe, void and hyperverse,. It was even argued to be affective on the ranked top five most powerful characters in existence. The attack potency was beyond the realm of any reality that angels and demons could ever calculate. Even by that destructive power of level, Caprins ability would work on that attack too.

The fifteenth duplicate of Caprin and a angry BWF, was ready to give the bat some pain, and BWF blasted Caprin to a place that was billions of years' worth of torment and Caprin came out of it fine.

"Shoot, I thought it would work this time, but I've got more in store for your death, you blind prostitute of Eogo! You are blind right?" Questioned BWF, who was waiting for an answer from Caprin, but didn't get any. Even though Caprin didn't answer, it is true that Caprin usually fights his opponents blinded, with himself combating BWF as an example.

"Okay silent school girl, it's time to put a stop to your goal in serving Eogo once and for all." Shouted a serious sound BWF.

Both Caprin and BWF united their duplicates into one being that cover a universe larger than an average universe into one being.

Caprin blasted an energy of letters spelling them, us, and why? towards BWF which paralyzed BWF in the process.

(It should be noted that Eogo can do what Caprin and BWF can do easily.)

Meanwhile with Zeth.

Limping away from Iaintyobuddy as much as possible, Zeth searched everywhere on top of the building for a way to drive. He saw an aircraft vehicle built for one person, and that one person was an anthropomorphic cat, with a leather coat and black pants. When Zeth was right in front of the cat, he ripped the cat's pockets out to get the keys and pushed him away. But not too hard, because he didn't want to injure the person. Going inside the vehicle was like going inside a typical small plane with the only difference being that it looked more futuristic and cyberpunk like. When Zeth got in the vehicle, he started to fly it, and flew up high away from Iaintyobuddy. Helicopters of the Insintation were coming and blasted mega rounds of minigun bullets towards the plane.

Iaintyobuddy was very happy, he smiled at the sight of the helicopters firing at Zeth, until he vomited out Elargarious.

Elargarious was coughing out ascites (pronounced ay-site-eez) from being drowned in the fluids of Iaintyobuddy and kicked the giant Hippo-potamus right on the bottom of his testicles. Iaintyobuddy gasped at first, and then laughed like a child being tickled.

"Blast you! You fat numbnut! You ruined my focus taking down Zeth!" Exclaimed an angry Elargarious who was about to hit Iaintyobuddy again, until Iaintyobuddy pointed at the sky saying. "Look birdy, it's a comic book hero!"

Elargarious growled at Iaintyobuddy for him saying that, and then more minigun sounds were heard. with his intention to see what was going on. When he saw helicopters trying to take down a one-person plane, he smiled and said. "That should do it."

As Zeth was flying from the bullets, the best as he could, he flew down to about fifty feet, closer to the roads with everyone looking astonished at what was happening. Two more helicopters arrived, with bazookas and miniguns ready to fire. Zeth's face was looking strenuous, with eyes wide open, and teeth were showing clenched together. Zeths hands were tightened, and sweaty. The cat-rat was feeling horrible, throughout, what was happening to him this night, from a usual spiritual influence of good and evil, to fighting the secondary big bad, and going down horror like stairs, being chased by a fat hippopotamus, a solipsism bird and helicopters. It just couldn't get any worse for him, two missiles from the bazookas hit the left wing of the plane he was flying in. The plane began to descend, and Zeth knew there was nothing he could do to prevent it. He chose to do a very risky stunt within the process of the plane's descent. Right at the very last second of impact, Zeth jumped off the plane from behind. When the plane crashed on impacted the road, the explosion from it sent Zeth flying over seventy feet into the air.

Zeth crash landed onto the front glass of a trailer vehicle, which got the anthropomorphic bear driver, who wore a green shirt and black pants knocked out on impact. The trailer vehicle was moving around recklessly. Zeth was seriously feeling quite out of it, but knew he had to react fast and take over the steering wheel. Zeth quickly placed the unconscious anthropomorphic bear driver on the right side of the vehicle, so that he could take the wheel. When Zeth managed to have control of the vehicle. Swat vehicles came racing towards him, with speeds of over 500 MPH. Zeth drove at full speed on the road, but the swat vehicles were catching up to him. Swat fired their ammunition at the trailer vehicle, which caused a lot of damage to it. More swat vehicles came in and rammed onto the trailer vehicle, which caused it to tilt a bit.

Swat team members with silver armor clothing, black armored pants, and a helmet with the front being black hard glass, and the back of it being silver football helmet shaped. These swat members were gliding down to the trailer vehicle with mechanical bat wings on their backs.

One member broke through the glass of the door that was next to Zeth and in doing so the swat member kicked Zeth on the neck. The swat member grabbed Zeth, while attempting to do more hits on him. Because Zeth used his left fist, he did a few punches on the front part of the helmet of the swat member, which he managed to easily break and severely damage the face. The swat member screamed in pain at what Zeth did. Zeth grabbed the swat members grenades and smoke bombs and threw the swat member out of the broken glass window. More swat members came down on the trailer in attempt to catch Zeth from behind. By a lucky guess, Zeth assumed this would happen and threw some of the grenades at the trailer, which blew off from the vehicle. This gave him more speed in driving, because the weight of the trailer was fully gone from the vehicle. However, even though he's gained more speed, the swat vehicles were still faster than the vehicle he was driving.

Zeth took a sharp turn to the left of the road, and into a tunnel of a bridge. The swat vehicles were driving in the distance in front of him.

Zeth had to think fast in this situation and threw the remaining bomb towards the swat members in front of him and threw smoke bombs at the swat vehicles behind him. The timing of this was at the very last second of the explosion force, which almost hit him on impact.

In this moment, Zeth was about to do something even more risky, he stopped the vehicle and jumped on the front of a swat vehicle that was behind him. The driver of the swat vehicle weaved on the road, and Zeth kept punching the glass wall, trying to break it. It was much harder than bulletproof glass, and Zeth failed to punch through it. Then the swat driver pressed his foot on the brake which sent Zeth flying backwards into the air, and he went past the burnt vehicles he blew up with a grenade. There he saw a weapon that was more powerful than a bazooka. It was 3'10" long, it looked like a gun and Zeth knew what it was. Zeth picked it up and almost at the very last second, with the swat vehicle getting twenty feet closer to Zeth, he blasted the front glass of the vehicle, and jumped in the swat vehicle. Zeths legs were poorly positioned on the front seats of the vehicle, and when the backseat swat member tried to shoot him, Zeth took the gun, snapped it in two and punched the backseat driver. The two other swat members were on the front seat with Zeth, and Zeth strangled the swat members on the front seats, but the one in the backseat elbow slammed Zeths nose, which caused him to let go of the driver but not the one next to him. On the right side of the swat vehicle, Zeth squeezed the right front seat swat members throat so hard, that it was to the point of the neck bleeding.

However, he was still getting punched by the one in front of him, and while the swat vehicle was moving recklessly the driver was regaining breath from being strangled by Zeth.

Zeth had to think fast, he then ripped off the adams apple of the backseat swat member he was strangling, dodged the back-seat swat members right arm punch and bent the entire arm in two. Zeth then grabbed the head of the driver and was about to snap his neck but the driver weaved from right to left, which made Zeth move almost to the front seat of the vehicle.

Zeth held his position on the right seat and was about to stop the vehicle for the swat members to get him, but Zeth grabbed the gun from the dead right front seat swat member, killed the driver with the gun, and kicked him out of the vehicle so that he could drive the swat vehicle. As he managed to drive in the streets of the city, lightning strikes blasted a thousand to ten thousand-foot buildings to the ground.

When Zeth looked up, he saw a giant hurricane in the sky with lightning strikes larger than a star. Although those lightning strikes were high up in the sky, the smaller ones were the ones that hit the ground. They were around the size of the world trade center, though progressively these lightning strikes were getting a bit larger, but over time, it grew larger and hotter with Zeth feeling the heat in the distance. Then strangely enough it felt cold, and Zeth felt a presence of some sort, with him, something that felt like it was a great aid to him. Zeth also noticed a partially red and icy circle, with it being seen through at first, like looking at a ghost in a way, but overtime the red and ice covered the road and was later blasted by a bolt of lightning.

Zeth saw more partially red and icy circles, which were eventually blasted by lightning strikes and something in the distance was running behind him. Zeth's eyes looked focused at the rearview mirror of the swat vehicle, and what he saw running towards him was a bird baby.

This is an enemy Zeth knew he couldn't fight in combat, it was a bird baby and it was capable of killing Zeth easily. The bird baby picked up a 4,500-foot-tall building with a width being 1,250 feet and threw it at Zeth. Just in the nick of time, before the building fell on top of Zeth, he took a swift turn to his left. The bird baby with a single punch, destroyed the building and was catching up with Zeth.

Zeth knew he had to think of something fast, before the bird baby could catch up to him and he thought about the lightning strikes that come from two characters who were far above the attack potency of a gamma ray burst and a VY Canis Majoris supernova.

Could it be possible that the lightning strikes from them could destroy or at least damage the bird baby? Then again, it didn't explode in a range of a mountain, however just because something doesn't make range in its attack potency, doesn't mean it cannot reach its attack potency. Therefore, Zeth is going to take the risk, but how was he going to do it? If Zeth was going into the heat of it, he'd likely disintegrate into ashes, and if he went into the ice, he'd freeze to death.

"Hey dude, who likes a relative of mine, can you hear me?" Said the echoed voice of BWF telepathically speaking to Zeth.

"Yes, I can, and need your help" Said Zeth

"I've set the temperature of the red and icy circles for your comfort, yah know i can do it, now get that stupid bird in there, before i change my mind" Exclaimed BWF After the telepathic information was over, Zeth knew the bird baby wouldn't be fooled into getting blasted by a lightning strike, but wondered if something from this vehicle could help him find a way to shut it down. Obviously, it would be temporary, since the guys running the bird baby would be suspicious as to who's controlling it. Since it is likely that the swat members might have something to do with the bird baby, they are affiliated with the Insintations military, Zeth might can find a way to control it.

In Zeths studies, the swat members carry a recording device that records what they do, which can give Zeth the advantage in figuring out how to stop it. Zeth's mind was racing as to who could possess this knowledge, and couldn't waste time by choosing a second, and at first thought the driver could be, but realized it's more likely to be the backseat swat member, and why could it be true? It's because that swat member was likely to be the most talented one, the backseat swat member had the most advantage in hitting Zeth, with the others easily being taken down, but not that one. It is kind of at least un-predictable because usually when you watch an action movie, it shows the guys doing the most action on the front seat and less on the backseat. Or at least that's from Zeth's perspectives of it. In less than a second, Zeth grabbed the dead body of the swat member, and checked for any recordings, found one and pressed the play button to play the recording.

"Carl, told us to press 6-3-7-3 on the buttons of the right door of the vehicle to activate the bird baby, and press 8-3-5 to turn it off, got it?"

Exclaimed the swat member. "We got it!" Said one of the swat members. "Good, recording." Said the swat member.

Zeth was about to press the buttons, but chose not to do it just yet, until he gets in the right position of being blasted by lightning. Zeth saw a huge partially red and iced circle on a town square and he drove straight towards it, with the bird baby coming in very close to him.

As Zeth made it in the partially red and icy circle, the bird baby was an inch behind him. He pressed 8-3-5 on the right door of the vehicle, which caused the bird baby's eyes to turn black and it completely stopped. Zeth drove the vehicle a foot closer and he got out of the vehicle and ran away from the partially red and icy circle. The reason why Zeth did this, is because he did not want them to use the vehicle as a possible trace to find him. As Zeth was running around to find a vehicle that wasn't swat, he saw a motorcycle, with a body crushed by pieces of a building, and he saw keys right next to the blood of the flattened body.

As Zeth was the closest to touching the keys, he felt something that felt like the aftermath of a disturbance, something that was clear but not really in a way of peace or calm natured. It was a strong feeling that sored around and within his spirit, everyone could feel it, Drofred, Elargarious, Iaintyobuddy, the swat members, and even Caprin and BWF felt it too. Despite showing a serious tightened mouth, Zeth's eyes were excited yet fearful of what he was feeling and said in a cautious tone.

"Lincent"

Meanwhile with Lincent

Buried underneath debris, Lincent was all wounded and almost completely knocked out from surviving transhumanist Drofred. Lincent's mind was out of focus, feeling dizzy and thinking randomly, with her mind saying. "Zeth, David, and…" Lincent couldn't think straight. Overwhelmed she was beginning to pass out.

Lincent groaning and moaning from the pain felt inside her was great, and she couldn't squirm, or move either because of the rubble on top of her. The pressure and the weight were getting close to crushing Lincents body, the sounds of her ever struggling to yell was faint, with a few squeaks and squeals. Slowly fading into sleep, a darkness was coming for Lincent, and when darkness fully shrouded, her eyes closed. In the darkness, blue blood dripped down like a cold morning. Wind sounds were in reverse, Lincent felt like she was not wearing clothes outside in a winter time season. Her body was cold.

Strangely enough, Lincent did not react to the cold at all like that.

Uncertainty courses down in Lincents thinking of all of this, with wondering what in the world was going on, and yet nothing. Lincent tried to call out to someone for help but nothing came from the sound of her voice, which gave a nervous gut-wrenching feeling inside of her. Lincent has seen horrible things in her life, however that doesn't mean she can't be afraid now and then. Lincents eyes looked focused into paying attention to her surroundings however what was scary about this is the question of what is surrounding her?

Is it a mind-rape of some sort? A monster of foul symbolism?

Or is it just her in a passed-out state? The issue with the subject of being in a passed-out state is that, this didn't feel like one. It felt more like the blackness of an unfinished job. It was as if this dark place was something Lincent could have sworn, that she had been to before, but couldn't put her finger on it. It was like being a negative dimensional world, a place that shouldn't exist, yet somehow, and even by those standards, it doesn't at all.

This all made Lincent panic at what was happening, the presence of evil that is. Nothing was triggering an alarm in her head. Lincent wanted to scream out for help, yet nothing was heard, the volume surrounding her was muted, meaning no sound could be heard. Lincent couldn't even hear her own thoughts which caused her heart to pound heavy and slow.

This place, which is purely abandoned, seems like a place that a nihilist would love a non-existence, but a non-existence that is beyond any concept of non-existence, being that it could be where all have been to before. Lincent tried fighting this, while yelling with all she had, and still no sound could be heard. Then a voice that sounded like Zeth was heard saying ….. "Lincent!"

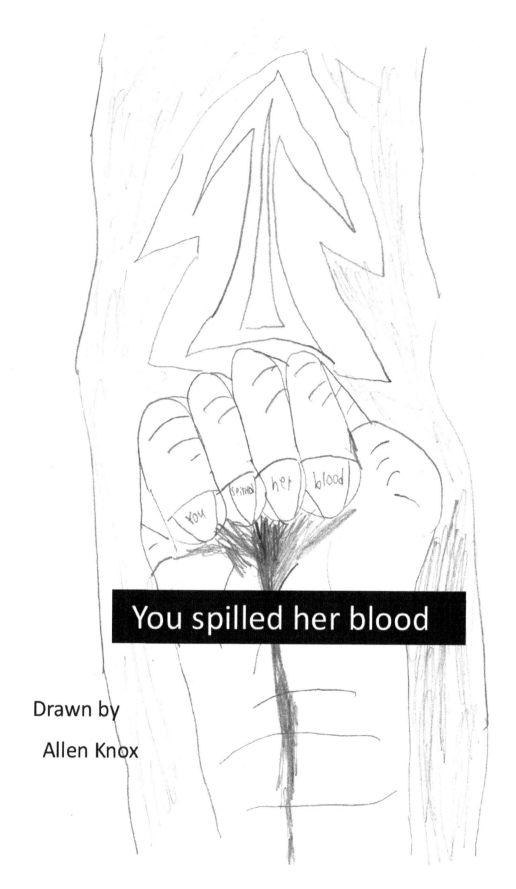

You spilled her blood

Drawn by

Allen Knox

Rubbles of the building that were on top of Lincent were being picked up by Zeth, and when Zeth saw Lincent, her eyes were closed with mouth opened like a dead person. Zeth got Lincent out of the rubble, and with his right hand he held her around the back, to comfort her. This caused great fear in Zeth. What was happening to Lincent, made Zeth very angry.

"Lincent, are you?!? Lincent! LINCE..!!" He cries out.

Before Zeth yells all the way, he remembered that he needed to keep quiet, and not letting anyone who's affiliated with the Insintation hear him. Zeth heard an intercom throughout the neighborhood which was Elargarious saying. "Zeth, you may have escaped from us this time, but soon that old story of escaping won't last much longer, and I will find you Zeth, and it will be very soon."

Zeth while holding Lincent was furious over Elargarious. He gave a very angry facial expression. He knew, what he was planning to do.

"I'm the one who's going to find you" Exclaimed a very hateful sounding Zeth.

THE LOVELY CLOUDS

Insintation country map

CHAPTER 8

Under The Rabbit Skin

IN A GRASSY knoll during the night time, BWF saw anthropomorphic people who glowed bright blood red, he saw himself amongst Lincent and Zeth that were blue. Out of a strange and unusual reaction, BWF, Zeth, and Lincent charged after the red anthropomorphic people whose faces turned into monstrous images. When BWF, Zeth, and Lincent slew the red anthropomorphic, people with swords, cheered in excitement of what they, the trio had just accomplished.

Zeth picked up Lincent and spun her around with joy of their achievement. When Zeth, put Lincent back down, something odd was happening with Zeth, and he looked like he was about to vomit.

Lincent was very worried about the sight of Zeth but didn't say anything. The look that Zeth gave to Lincent was the look of someone saying … 'I.. I don't feel so well,' and Zeth was beginning to shake.

Lincent held onto Zeth, with eyes appearing as if she was losing hope, but everywhere else of her facial expression said otherwise, which gestured hope for Zeth's well-being.

Zeths facial expression was the look of feeling worthless to Lincent, it was an appearance of sadness, and defeat, it was like as if he was dying.

Lincent stared directly into Zeth's eyes, her concern was obviously on a deeper level, letting him know that there was more in the future to look forward to. A world where people are longing to be happy, a world where pain and sorrow are officially gone.

This is what they agreed to be a part of. This is what made Zeth feel a bit more optimistic on the topic of the future. Lincent, kept trying to remind Zeth of this, multiple times. He knew it was a lot better than what the Insination are doing, leading the world into destruction.

Zeths face was starting to appear strained, and he was feeling new kinds of hurt, that felt like parasites inside his body.

Lincent was feeling it too and was shaking badly from it.

"Nothing I can't handle, as long as I'm around, no one's going to lose their lives, I can do anything." Exclaimed a confident BWF

"Your overconfidence is going to get us slaughtered, we're going to need help from the people who research this, and I'm not saying your worthless, in figuring things out, but our best hope is getting a doctor who knows about this." Exclaimed Lincent who was holding her body tightly while the pain started taking over. Zeth quickly held onto Lincent, to give her some warmth, even if he wasn't that warm, he still wanted to hold onto her.

"You bad baby makers, that love assuming! I'm going to screw everything, when I can do anything, I can conquer any villain, even Eogo, I'm getting stronger, I'm a perfect hero, no one's going to perish under my watch, not even Pakpao, I'm the best that no one can ever reach, so suck it up, and let me heal you." Exclaimed an arrogant BWF.

"No" Exclaimed a serious Lincent

"Your just ashamed of how great I am, I'm the one who's progressing the future, and when I reach beyond everyone, no one will top my mad skill'z and I will be the true savior of this world!" Said a self-righteous BWF.

Lincent and Zeth looked fed up with BWFs ego. He talks big about himself. Also, by the look in their eyes there was sadness over BWF not letting his view go on getting the better of himself.

"Quit trying to be my parents, damn it! None of you two, will ever be fit to be my parental guardians." Cried out a harsh BWF.

This statement, made Lincent sad, knowing that BWF plays a similar role of Jerico who wants to be greater than the one who is above everyone. Zeth however was displeased and was mad about what BWF was saying to Lincent. Zeth wanted to punch BWF on the face, but for some reason he couldn't put himself to do it.

"Let me heal yah, you dumb smucks!" Yelled BWF who was glowing bright red.

Lincent moved her head back and forth sideways, gesturing a 'no' to BWF, this made BWF mad and he ran towards both Lincent and Zeth who held each other tight in fear of what BWF might do to them.

When BWF was less than a foot away from Zeth and Lincent, he raised his right wrist being ready to swat at them, but his left hand grabbed his right wrist, which was turning gray for some reason, with some gray fur sticking out of his left wrist.

It seemed as if the gray hand was getting the upper hand until slithering red lines from the red hand were latched onto the gray hand, spawning more red lines on the gray hand, forming it back into glowing red.

BWF swatted Zeth on the face, which left marks of red slithering lines on him, turning Zeth into a red demonic monster of some sort, and appeared to be wearing a red demonic mask.

Lincent, looked at Zeth with an upset expression on her face, like the kind of expression a girl would give after having a mental breakdown.

BWF swatted at Lincents face, which quickly turned her into a red monster, with black eyes, and horns on the back of her head.

Zeth's belly button spewed out leeches with red eyes, bat ears and bat wings. These leeches breathed out blood red that created a formation, showing a body fighting a goat that is rammed the baby with its horns. The baby at first was fighting off the goat, but eventually the goat did one last hit on the baby, which caused a huge burst of ashes to come from the flames. The ashes and flames covered Zeth's entire body, and the ashes and flames showed a curly haired cat-rat child, with cat ears, cat whiskers and a mouse tail. The child shot out monsters from its hands, a shadow of a roped woman was being tortured by the child who was transforming into worms, rubbing around the roped woman's body. Slime was coming out from all over the worm's bodies, and what came out of the worms, was miniature mazes with dots moving inside them.

This temporarily made the woman's body split into multiple pieces, and she was getting smaller and smaller. When the woman got into the hole, images of gangs, crime lords, politicians, scientist, tyrants, bad parent images of committed sins were being shown from the ashes and the flames. The ashes and the flames spun around like a tornado with the difference being that it's shaped zig zag. When the zigzagging tornado blew away a skinless cat-rat with dry eyeballs appeared.

The skinless cat-rat jumped after Lincent, but Lincent in literally no time, grabbed the skinless cat-rats throat and snapped his neck. BWF screamed in pain and gray colors were being expelled from him, and Lincent in no time was right in front of him. Flashes of BWF being in the real world, were showing snake bat heads of Caprin biting BWF.

Then flashes of BWF back in the non-real world showed Lincents appearance turning back to normal but she was struggling in doing so.

Lincents fingers held on to her face, she pulled her skin and screeched in terror at what Caprin was doing. Flashes of the real world were back, with BWF being covered and bitten by snake bat heads of Caprin. The brightness of BWF, was flashing off, showing his true form. With arms that were furry gray, black torn pants, and the Insintation logo with a X on it. The flashes in the non-real-world showed a red bird in a female wedding dress being crushed by a giant statue of a male with a black suit, whose face was covered by darkness. BWF's hands twitched in a angry state, this was something that he took as an insult, and attempted to destroy the giant statue, but when he first touched the suit, BWF was zapped into another world, that had blue skies with no land or sun. In the distance in front of BWF, Caprin was chewing pieces of Pakpaos belly, and when the pieces of the inside parts of the belly were falling down from a punched hole in her back, the pieces fell down to the bottom of the sky, and then the pieces shaped into a clock, and a rabbits fist punched through it and grabbed BWFs face. Flashes of BWF in the real world was being shown, his face squeezed by Caprin's strange formations of many kinds of shapes. A snake, a dragon, an elephant, a tiger, and many more appeared.

Dark shadowy shape forms were moving around, and gave a tightened squeeze, to BWFs body. Then a spinning giant black chainsaw was ready to slice BWFs body in half. Flashes returned once more, but this time, it showed anthropomorphic people of all ages, babies, kids, teenagers, young adults, middle age, and the elderly, who were in a purple cake with pink icing. On the dead center of the cake, showed half of a body of a cat-rat, only showing its legs, shoes, and dark green pants. There was a mouse tail of the person whose body was chopped in half by the sword Xifos Gia Midenismo, which was right in front of the top bottom half of the body.

Giant, bright purple glowing hands, grabbed the cake, and threw pieces of it at BWF, which somehow caused his mind to feel the expression, of people suffering, and dying by seemingly no one causing it. Storms, diseases, accidents, all of these apparently had no enemies causing this, neither was an inner conflict doing this either.

Suddenly all the images of these events happening were spinning around. It was something or someone from the top, that was brighter than the sun. When BWF was staring at it, Caprin was surrounded by darkness, and was right under BWF. Dark energy was coming out of Caprin, and onto BWF, who was transforming into a black shadowy Jackalope, with red dragon wings. BWF gave an angry expression with his Jackalope face, and BWF flew up towards the bright figure. Red teeth were shown from BWF who was doing everything he could to reach the bright figure until Lincent appeared from above and reached out with her hand to get BWF. At first BWF refused to get close to her and hissed with demonic sounds added with it. Lincent was coming closer to BWF with a face wanting him to not be overwhelmed by Caprins dark spiritual powers upon him. BWF was afraid of grabbing her hand, he felt consumed by Caprins darkness, but the more he saw Lincent who encouraged him to beat this darkness, it made him feel ready to grab a hold of her hand. When BWF's right hand reached out to Lincent, his right arm turned furry gray, and Lincent began to drag him away from Caprin, until Caprin grabbed a hold of him. Lincent had alot of difficulty in lifting BWF up and Caprin was creating black veins on BWFs furry arm. Caprin was holding onto BWF's legs so tightly that he began to bleed.

BWF yelled in pain at what Caprin was doing to him, Lincent was crying over the overpowering struggle, and Caprin gave more of an angry demonic face while trying to drag BWF down. Then another hand appeared and grabbed a hold of BWF. Lincent looked to her side to see who it was, and it was Zeth Drastic helping her lift up BWF from the darkness and into the light. Caprin, still kept pulling BWF back to him, creating a tug a war challenge for Zeth and Lincent. Zeth and Lincent were determined to save BWF from

Caprins clutches and bring him into the light. Eventually, they were gaining the upper hand and fully lifted BWF into the light. BWFs true appearance was fully shown, and it was a anthropomorphic rabbit, who wore a black mask that covered his left eye, with stitches around it to make it stay on his face. He has on the shirt and pants he wore when fighting Caprin, and is now grown up, with the height of 5'8, rabbit ears, and red eyes. This character is David.

"I still think I can save everyone, even Pakpao the elderly lover of the arguably biggest hypocrite of all time, Nortric." Exclaimed an ignorant David. Zeth and Lincent sighed over David, still not getting the idea that he can't save everyone knowing how dangerous the Insintation is. A likely death or something horrific will happen soon in the future. Zeth and Lincent's facial expressions were of sadness, knowing that David still has a lot to learn in defeating the enemy.

"It won't be any issue, I promise" yells out a confident and foolish David.

Meanwhile with Elargarious.

Outside of the black tank, which was larger than a pharmacy building, and had the red Insintation goat emblem on the front, left, right, and back side of the tank wrapped around it. The inside of this tank had red radar systems, a few swat members inside wore black diamond armor on their body, arms, and legs. Inside the center of the tank was Elargarious sitting on a black diamond throne with sapphire cubes on top of it. Elargarious closed his eyes, putting himself in a thought process of who he has become, and other strange things.

"What a loss, or was it? Wrodsord has been known to die on multiple occasions. He was probably just making an analysis on Zeth Drastic, or to test himself even further in overcoming death in his way. My son Carl sure does have an interest in his desire for immortality. I bet even Baxter Drastic, aka Drofred is learning some things on the path of immortality though transhumanism. I myself don't need transhumanism or anything from that priest birds 'wachings' in 'living forever.' For that I am the eternal, I must be, it cannot be a coincidence on why I specifically have this point of view 'and this point of view alone.' There must be something about my very own existence in seeing things by my perspective, I must not feel alone on the matter, but feel like a father of some sort to my created children of whom I suppressed my intelligence and power for, creating a boundary for myself. But how I am going to get it back? Oh, crap the panic is coming out of me, this can't get me to be shaken. The nerves of my wellbeing need to stay intact and not freak out over the truth of the destiny that I must take place to forever."

"No, no, please don't let it happen, this can't happen, the realization of solipsism is a revelation from God, which is me, I am the son of God, that's why I have this one directional point of view, and everyone else are my children. They're not people testing me, I'm not some endless infinite experiment going into infinite experiment of comprehensive reality, past any kind of reality in existence, never being free from myself which is the only one to ever exist. Even if I do die, I'll come back and eventually my true powers shall return and destroy who opposes their creator of everything and everyone."

"Nnnaaahh, no, damn it please, no, my blow out, my alarm trigger of skull and body, it's gonna blow! Just stay positioned, self-control STAY POSITIONED! Don't crumble! Please, this has been destroying my foundation as a perfect creator. The solipsism panic, as a perfect creator, the solipsism panic, from the time of, which I appreciate the masses calling it 'Afternoon Solipsism'. It in such a magnificent piece in time of the all-powerful creator Elargarious knowing his purpose for the world, all the little children who are faithful and believeth in me all the way, become saints in the kingdom of Elargarious. Those short moments of my childhood were and will soon be forever more the greatest of better for all eternity. Then sunset of my solipsism came, and it was a feeling of mixture, should I be omni-benevolent? Because there are wicked souls who completely deny myself as their maker, even to the point of battling me, they are sewage cow ding dongs, people or sick freaks like them have zero placement in my perfected world, I can see many of them who oppose the order of the creator, with a thought provoking one that is Zeth Drastic." Elargarious pauses and then continues… "A traitorous family member, a deceitful rat desiring cheese. I hate him, he humiliated me in causing my solipsism to panic in front of everybody. Using spiritual energy on my mind, this amplified my panic attacks uncontrollably, losing focus in fighting and getting knocked out. Though Zeth had to get help from Lincent in a MLVFG/many lesser versus fewer greater fight, against my superior power, and Zeth wasn't the first one to do something similar like this. I remember when my supposed father sowed the seeds of solipsism in my mind, but the foolish sperm father of mine Nortric, of whom I have started to question being my sperm father because I surely must have been born of a virgin without sperm. I don't believe in any of the so-called confirmed test of him being my father, but my solipsism is enough to show that I'm non-sperm virgin born. Sure, I'm recognized by everyone else as him being my dad and showing Nortrics sperm go into the egg of my mother, is something that I consider to be special effects junk. What's sad is that my mother even says that Nortric is my biological father. I was reliant in existing by his own sperm. However, I think she knows the honesty of truth within such foul sperm story of a man who is trying to pull a super twisted ideal in destroying the creator of everything. Maybe I should bet, that even if Nortric didn't use such energy on me, I would Eventually find out who I am, and destroy the wolves, and bring my sheep into their holy land of 'praising and grazing' their all-mighty creator, which is me, Nortric was trying to get my enemies into thinking that Nortric poisoned my mind. If anyone sighs and rolls their eyes at my statement, they will have their necks clawed off and thrown into the fire pits of Hades. That's what Nortric was trying to do, and he succeeded for the time, or did he? Non the less, he's a filthy fake sperm non-daddy!

Such pathetic behavior of a man, who was admired by Eogo, who seeks to betray me. I remember when I fought both Zeth and Lincent, and how they tried to falsely inform and accuse me that I'm creating an illusion with the establishment of my character." Elargarious was not finished. "How rude of them making a claim that became a slander of the ocean being polluted, their food and drinks that are not fruits or clear water, but drugs and wine. They hurt me with tremendous tearing of the spirit of Elargarious. Zeth thinks he can defeat me in the dark, of that type of solipsism. It always made me feel like as if I'm the nightmare of my revelation, the 'always-have-been-God-inheritance' was a feeling that wasn't good. It felt so uncomfortable, the madness of my mind racing was a vortex of screaming high pitch, yelling out God, God! Help me God! God! Where are you!?! Help me! God! Gaawwwd! Oh, what a hell driven moment of my release of berserk and shivering behavior. I don't want to ever go back to it again, for this ideology is not such self-destructive to humanity, if it's only me who carries this ideology to only me alone. The 'not-so-alone', Because I have children, and people say that the creator wasn't lonely in making us, that he just wanted us. I refuse to believe it, I deny it, and must put a Gosh durned law to it. Yes … I blasphemed myself, because I can do whatever I the fuzz want to. As the creator I can counteract any contradiction by just my own thoughts. Yes, my kids, it is true, and I know your hearing me paraphrase with an excellent paragraph upon you all.

The wicked must be deafened and dead to the lake of burning sulfur.

Critics of films have a warmed-up tendency in doing such sad things, but some of those of whom their criticizing could be my children, and I don't like them bullying my constructed animatronics or even me for that matter. They must not dare even have a 'not-should-be' predestined thought of getting on my case for my doings. My will is incorruptible, no one has reached up to a mastery of orchestrated creation like mine. The same goes for Jerico, Savage, and Fabast, who believe they can rise above the true powers that I wield over them. Sadly, their mindset has led to never reaching my tier system. My level is incomprehensible. Even in the non-hundred percent of the scaling. I know many things, I know that Pillar Dark IX/Crigs crown maybe the most sinister and dangerous, mind rape super weapon in all of existence." Elargarious wasn't finished…. "Sight, feel, comprehension, burden, them, us, and why, conscious, sub-conscious, unconscious, deception of the two beasts, x marked sperm, and tangled black spiked forward sperm, power for others and power for self. I discovered these key things by my own perception, that verdamnt's sayings of them, swearing to the establishments of evil. This was not of them showing me, but of myself with supreme predestination of which I am supreme in being above. Just like the time of the true father which is the all-powerful creator which is me. I am the son of which is still me that churches do an overly complicated job in describing. I hope by me saying this out loud, that people don't call me an artist of contradiction, because 'If-you-think-about-consideration' was put to the test of noticing simplicity then it turns it simple. Your just not thinking hard enough. or is that your saying more towards complexity than simplicity, and you've got to think soft enough. 'ah ha soft enough. I creator of everything who must not feel lonely have established a creation with web lines of predestination to which I am above in full control and taking full control of the outer levels of all concept in writing literature/fiction/all sorts of buck oh! 'This somehow exists with predestination the 'oh Hell' even the designer of the omni verse, designer of all! Yes, my composition is too good, to NOT be true. My knowledge sees the dark secrets that Lincent possesses. All that weird junk. How else would she have a kid to be so powerful to fight Caprin? Was there not tales of her being connected to some nut-jobby witches who have some voodoo wickedness to do with her? Why are people saying she's so old and forgets important vague things? Maybe she and I have something in common. I know I have forgotten my true intellect. I was progressing into the life of glorious riding. But ... yeah, those Lincent stories are, well, their, something. Else, especially with Sams interest in her." Elargarious stops, breathes and continues.

"For some reason, it might not even be sexual, but something very personal to him, but what the fudge of verdamnt was it? Was it something like the disruption that many of us felt within a large range? And I mean a very large spectrum of feeling. You can sense it, it's out of this world. Maybe even literally, of darkness being the opposite of power, which is very powerful, and I heard rumors of Crig having some kind of liking to her. Now that's fascinating, but back to Sam. Like I said it's quite different, or strange showing of him being urged to be near her and claims that it's just him wanting to help the good guys, but surely there's a more legitimate and deeper underground tunnel to his unstable character." Elargarious didn't stop there. He continues with...

"Sure, the wife of his father Nortric was there, but there was something about her, that intrigued him. There were some sentences that the Judgmisspast put out, being about the energy connection they have. Kind of like Lincent's son David, he has a connection, of all many sorts of spiritual energies, especially the black of its kind. And what is with the Judgmisspast fascination of Zeth and Lincent? She said, she was informed of them being destined to be together. Never let anyone that I know of, have any knowledge of who informed her. Maybe it's just the Judgmisspast being coco crazy as usual. I strongly feel it needs to be questioned, as to why the curious aspect of Lincent's connection to the storyline. Fancy them with such webs in a center place, with Caprins interest in slaying a dying redbird. like what's the deal with those two? I don't see why we should even care about her, since she's to the point of almost being dead. Why even bother? Unless, Possibly? Nope that can't be true, now what do I have to remember with my returning omniscient. Oh yeah! Carl being my kid, like he is my biological son, that is a confirmation that I cannot deny. I regret losing his mother, my own son has been yearning for such happiness but sadly, such love from a mother has been departed from him. It is so much of a high degree of absence from a mother warmth, that the absence is unbearably high." "I should of never, made that bet of me doing everything, and beating the opponent in a higher score of course. And by me doing it, she lives." Elargarious is adamant. "Failure in doing so would result to her being one of the Judgmisspast and Iaintyobuddys wives. And I failed the test, which led to her unimaginable torment. And it was all my fault! I should have said, Wait a second, I cannot admit failure, her hurting is part of my perfect plan in avoiding hurt. She will be free, if she's still alive that is. Although I do carry the path of immortality, forget Wrodsord, I'm the king of kings! I must get back on track with my omniscient. Yes, the gasp in excitement of the rabid land, the area of everything owned by the Tranpolies stirs up my omniscient." "But, that's off the topic of my endless number of cells processing my final league that shall return soon." Elargarious then confirms "No slanders should ever be suggested to the previous sentence. Verdamnt I am overcoming! No wait, I can't overload, I am beyond overloading and limitation."

"Thus, with those words shoved aside. I am thinking of the past, which should somehow in some positive optimistic solution of 'a-be-present' and future. But let's go back to the past, because I just forgot why present and future are even accountable? Verdamnt, that cannot happen, that's blasphemy to my very soul, which is infinite beyond the infinites being calculated. Oh, damn it! I need to get back on topic, what was the topic? No, I shouldn't question that, I'm born of a virgin without sperm, and came out of a nasty hole! Now that the thought process is returning to my marvelous abilities, and the topic of the paragraph is something super long, filled with letters and words being repeated in my mind. I am in a continued state that must be put to a halt and is about the ridiculous false claim of Crigs doom without bloom. A time of mostly silence with damnation becoming an adaption to humanity that became furries. The phrase of 'when they come from under the farewell shall be the family's greetings' even I the lord of all must admit, there's something that is going to become a relationship to a chaos without escape. Crigs crown is comparable to it. I wouldn't be surprised if it's more than comparable. The word comparable isn't even close to the highest relation of meaning of Crigs crown for the events that is yet to come. Every thought of it, really does make me my power weaker. I know what a gigantic shift in mindset is right? Who am I playing comedian with? Perhaps their right, maybe I'm one out of the trillions that is created like an individual, not seeing the main idea that everyone has their one and only point of view. And I probably need to retire. But there's always a percentage of the possibility of me being the one and only point of view. Or, I'm just some overly excited guy who needs to finally get a grip and take a chill pill over the matter that needs to be done."

"With my mind dismantling, another piece of memory just popped like a cat clawing a balloon in my skull. With the story being a case of what they did to Carl Drastic. They went way too far with dropping him in Eogo's blood. Or was it Apinbuls blood that he went into? If you ask me, the traits are similar, and Iaintyobuddy might have scooped some of his in that pool. The fat hippopotamus, with a dumb brain thinks he's above pain, and everyone should feel it but him. His rival makes a huge over-score to his belief motivated system of the fat hippopotamus pain on others. Who should really care about that hippo? Even by his duration, and inconsistent striking strength, and being greater than a birdbaby, withstanding and punching damage. He's just a dummy that needs to die and be forgotten." Elargarious was overwhelmed and falling short for words.

"Now back to the topic of what was happening with my son Carl, or maybe Carl is my daughter, who knows? I might hold this thought, if I remember it ...that is. But this topic upsets me, now my sons sorrow over wanting good, has been the result of him or her being warped by Apinbul and the Judgmisspast. I thought by doing another somewhat or entirely all-powerful feat against my opponent, that I would have been able to download it. It didn't result to this achievement in the slightest. I begged for them to put Carl in there, but as a part of the deal, and as much as I hate to admit it, I failed to fulfil the godlike feat. Which led to my son's darkness, for this world to be amplified horribly. My son hates me now and used to believe in me as the savior and deity of the omniverse. Now Carl sees me as a joke, someone to never ever be around with. I don't want to think about depressive information of my lover and son who could be my daughter. It makes me doubt myself as the divine being of 7/7. "Elargarious, stops and ponders further.

"I have another thought stored in memory that I didn't think about, Holy-in and wicked-out. Now those two, are technically the ones that have a freaky fun sense of wanting to depart from Eogo's fulfillment for Crig. Even being said to have a tendency of leaving too. Just like Innercist lighter side in leaving, which Caprin and Eogo forced to make us create clones of them, because of that white bird l am leaving her place with Eogos fulfillment."

"It might be possible that some others, could have a desire to leave their holder. Like the time when Savage was made, he created heliocentric universes, and outer space sized worlds. In those worlds. Savage became a messiah figure in taking down villains, that he created.

He helped others with his diverse universes. The stories of Savage with his created universes, possibly even hyperverses are totally bizarre and beyond comprehensive thought, except for me of course, or at least somehow that is. He wants to rule over Jerico, his 'Holder'. Goodness and good grief of heavens to Betsy, so much is popping out of my mind in this excitement. I need to re-establish these things, so that I can plan it better, like the gender secret of Carl, what the hell is that supposed to be? Why do Zeth and others mispronounce my name into Alargarious or to Alaygarious? Zeth claims there is a dangerous guy named Maskcat but who is Maskcat? There's no record or anything of this guy, not even people on Zeths team knows what he's talking about And I've got a thought of the bet I made with Caprin of me defeating Zeth which will grant all of land Insintation. But If I fail then he'll kill me, however failure won't happen because I'm reaching my peak."

"My peak, that is past ever, ever known in existence, so I'm going to die, I'm going to win, and will kill the unfaithful and disrespectful making of mine, who I breathe life into. And everyone should know that I possess the breath of life, and those who follow me shall have ever lasting life. It has been written in history of who I am, for that the creator so loved the world of sin. Yes sin, for that sin will grant more power, but to the education on my soul, which is him giving his only son to the world. So that everyone shall have eternal life. Not the Judgmisspast view on it, just greatness. When I breathed the life into Zeth, which was by the help of his sperm father and mother. Zeths development quickly grew up to be against me, the one who breathed the breath of life through the sperm as a result of his existence being made. Sure, his existence wasn't reliant on my sperm, but none the less, since I am the son of God. Life only comes from me, and yet Zeth defies the son of God, for the crimes that Zeth choose to commit, his name will not be written in the book of life, but in the book of death, and he will suffer forever and ever. Shoot me to dogs on fire, but my time is up on rethinking, I've got to be preoccupied on the goal that is at hand. Which is to take down Zeth Drastic. One other thing on mind. And it's Drofreds motives in establishing this world through his own electronic technology. Things became very steampunk and cyberpunk when Carl and Baxter Drastic were making things. They operate in their own competition that has made Insintation of what it is today, or tonight to be more specific. Baxter wants to step it up a notch, and with his transhumanist form, he has the power to destroy a city. However, Baxter has stated that his form has weaknesses inside Drofred headquarters, and I hope Zeth hasn't found the weakness yet. But the thing is that he probably already has discovered the secret through the help of the people who Aid him… And he already knows the vulnerability of how my weakness works. Which is a feeling of the dark night solipsism, that causes a berserk out of control freak out of me. But I've got to conquer my fears and face this fear of mine and kill Zeth Drastic." Elargarious rants and rants.

"Ohhh!!!! and I forgot one last thing, which is what Caprin is said to be doing behind my back, subtly making sure I stay with my belief. Personally, I find that hard to believe because not many spiritually influenced have learned doing it in secret. People who have awareness of such spiritual influence, surely are not so weak to the point of not realizing it, am I correct, oh well guess my drifting thoughts have expired, it's time for Baxter and I to have a bit of a chat." Elargarious then breathes.

Meanwhile with Zeth

In a neighborhood somewhere around the inside of land Insintation was a blue house, and Zeth held Lincent and took her inside. Thirty minutes later Zeth built up his gear to be ready for Elargarious and Drofred and brought gadgets. The first gadget was called 'the muscle ripper 1979', It was a suit that covers Zeths body and stretches his muscles up to the capacity of lifting the real-life world trade center that was destroyed in 2001. With this suit, one punch, or a single kick could destroy buildings up to the size of the world trade center. The second gadget was called 'Uber Weighted ball', which needs to be very carefully used because it's meant to impact pressure more than a hundred fifty times the weight of the world trade center. It also has chains tide to it, where when Zeth spins it, the ball crushes and rips apart everything on impact. This is when the moment of good timing is important pressing the button that activates its full strength.

The third gadget is a '75th Paward', a gadget that has been known to enhance combative speed, and possibly racing speed to over 75,000 punches and kicks per second. The biggest weakness, the first and third gadget is that 'the muscle ripper 1979' has its limits, and when using full power going past the maximum limit could strain Zeths body, and possibly destroy his entire body into pieces. As for the third gadget Paward, if Zeth stopped fighting from a nonstop continuous fight that is even a few minutes long, he might pass out or his arms and legs may be disabled. Though the degree to how badly damaged his arms and legs get, depends on the extent on how he uses it. In pronto reaction time, Zeth chose to drive a black armored truck, that was 5'10" wide, wheels 4'8" long, the length of the vehicle was 8'6", and it's height is 6'4 feet tall. Zeth started the vehicle and drove at full speed to the destination of where Elargarious and Drofred awaited. Zeth knew what they were up to, and had to put a stop to it, before it was too late. Almost at the same time and sometimes at the same time, Zeth thought about his goal to Elargarious and Drofred, but also thought about Lincent. While Zeth had to get this done, his mind on Lincent was like a flash of lightning. Zeth wants to make a future with Lincent, in a world of peace, and he wants to make up for all the wrongs he's done in the past. But after what Drofred did to Lincent, Zeth became enraged and furious over what has happened to her. Zeth wants to make Drofred pay for this, to the point of where he would never forget it. The other things Zeth had in mind about Lincent was trying to start a family with no big problem on the way. Zeth is urged to take the relationship much further than that, just being partners, but doesn't think Lincent wants to take it to that level. just because Zeth thinks Lincent won't raise the level of the relationship to something more, doesn't mean Lincents not going to either. As for Elargarious, Zeth had a hunch in knowing what Elargarious was trying to do. Whatever he could to achieve 'Godhood status' by considering Drofreds inventions as of the key, to the highest power. In truth, Elargarious is delusional, trying to use a mental defense mechanism in not having a panic attack or commit suicide from feeling alone. Him being the only one to exist, with everything else being artificial. Even though Zeth knows that Nortric had something to do with Elargarious solipsism, he's having trouble believing Nortric is all-out evil because of what Zeth and he went through together.

Everyone of Zeths friends suggest the possibility of Nortric being a sinister manipulator, but Zeth doesn't think this is true. Even people who were around with Nortric more than Zeth, claim he's a treacherous Drastic member that Eogo is using for his/her plan. People within Insintation are skeptical in trusting Nortric, there are also people who trust the Judgmisspast of all sinners more than Nortric. There is said to be a little bit of sympathy for Nortric, knowing that he had some struggles in having faith in the all-powerful being where whatever it is that can happen, just happens. It is very likely that Cressida Drastic will never forgive Nortric for what he has done but is internally challenged in wanting to kill him for his own false doings. Hardly ever, has post-distaste Nortric Cressida state this but she has claimed that she has seen a white strand of good energy coming out of him, and this was during the time of him committing his sins. Maybe Nortric is just caught in a dysfunctional situation and is trying to decipher with right and wrong. But, Nortric should be questioned for his true allegiance, the Insintation, the good of the people, or his own self needs. As Zeth almost reached to his destination, one last thing was captivating his mind, and it was about the slimy creature's statement being 'when they come from under, the farewell shall be the family's greetings'. Zeth knew what that could likely be. He felt deeply afraid of that statement. It is a statement that is about doom without bloom, where it all comes down to, and will likely be, of great loss of lives, by ending and horribly continued. So far from what's been seen, Zeth didn't even shake at such a scary build up, because it is probably going to happen, knowing how big of a deal the Insintation is, the worst that is yet to come will do a large amount of damage to all of existence. Crig's crown, the pillar dark IX, the star crown piece of Crig, is definitely a key factor to the doom without bloom and is quite possibly indestructible. Zeth managed to get in range of the sight of where Elargarious and Drofred were awaiting and they feel ready to face them.

Meanwhile with Lincent.

In a room with white paint and a lamp next to the bed that had blue and yellow striped sheets. Lincent was making raspy breathing noises and had an oxygen respiratory mask assisting her to breath. When the door opened, suddenly an elderly looking woman appears, with long gray hair, red eyes, cat ears, pink nose, and a mouse tail. This woman appeared very aged and looked as skinny as a dry broom-stick weighing only 65 pounds. As a matter of fact, this person does weigh 65 pounds, and her name is Cressida Drastic. This is the Pakpao from chapters 4-7, and she looked afraid of what has happened to Lincent.

Cressidas hands were shaking, both in fear and the result of her body aging. Cressida grabbed Lincents left arm as a sign of worry for her condition, and Cressida closed her eyes from over the sight of a girl who she cared for a lot. Cressida was scared to open her eyes, she didn't want to see Lincent hurt anymore and when she slowly opened her eyes, her cornea turned red from tears coming down to her cheeks. Cressida wants to believe in what Lincent is trying to do, which is to take away the sinful rotten hearts of spirits and make them "born a new" with a heart of kindness. But after seeing how far the non-repenting sinners would do to someone who wanted to save Zeths life, pressures of doubt in Cressida's mind is convincing those sinners to give up their ways and live a righteous life. Cressida knows that Lincent may have her struggles in forgiving sinners for their ways, but if they strive for repentance, she may come to consideration of accepting their apology. While Lincent is likely not to be close blood kin related to Cressida, that doesn't mean she's not family. In some ways Lincent is like a little sister to Cressida, they've been through so much together that Cressida didn't want to lose her, but is uncertain on how bad of the current state she is in. Cressida couldn't stand seeing Lincent being in the condition of dying state and looked up

Drawn by

Allen Knox

at the window in a devastated manner. As Cressida looked out the window, she hoped for Zeth to be gaining victory over Elargarious and Drofred and put an end to the Insination once and for all. Cressida knew she couldn't do it herself, because of how her body is dying and is getting close to death. Not only that, but Caprins got his eye on Cressida as a confirmed personal target for his kill list, why it's personal is yet to be known. Cressida is very aware of how close she is to death and knows it's only a very uncertain matter of time until it does happen, with being killed as an easy first thought. With examples to bring as evidence for the previous sentence is one, Cressida had multiple heart attacks. Two, Cressida had her body shut down and die once, and her soul almost left her body, which nearly resulted within a hair second close to an official death. Three, Cressida has cancer. Four, Cressida is reaching to the eventual killing of M.S. Five, during some battles Cressida was in, evil characters placed demonic curses of her life span being shortened greatly. Six Cressida also has been cursed by Caprin to have a life span no higher than a non-anthropomorphic dog, and she has reached past the maximum life of those animals. Seven, Cressida doing this. With Lincent being close to death, Cressida chose to give away some of her energy and cells to Lincent. This ability is called 'Sacrive-life' an ability that the user can give all their life energy and cells to someone or some of it, Cressida chose some of it. This caused Cressida to physically age even more and have some pain in her body that will be permanent until death. Lincent opened her eyes and saw Cressida's head and eyes rolling dizzy like. This made Lincent gently, but in quick reaction grab Cressidas arms and say in a frightened tone of voice.

"You shouldn't be doing this for me, I was the one who chose to risk my life for Zeth, what I was trying is do is save a life, not cost someone else's!" Not even David could stop the results of 'Sacrive-life' which puts Cressida even further past the maximum of what she is supposed to be in age. Lincent's mouth opened a little, the situation of the current state of Cressida Drastic was sad and she felt to help in fixing what she cannot fix.

"Llliccaent"!!! Exclaimed Cressida who was having trouble speaking to Lincent.

"Please don't exhaust yourself, you've done so much for me and I don't deserve it. It's you who should be rewarded, not me." Exclaimed an emotional Lincent who couldn't stand seeing Cressida risk her own life span to Lincent, because Cressida is family to her as well.

"The, the, thenn, rreewaard me innn hel helping Zeth." Said a stuttering dizzy, sickened, and weakened Cressida.

While Cressida's brain was getting weaker, she put as much as she possibly could in focusing in a one on one dialogue with Lincent. Lincent closed her mouth, eyes fully opened wide, but engaged in depth with every word Cressida was saying to her. They both knew that it would be unlikely for Zeth Drastic to do this alone, for that Drofred has become almost vastly too much for him to handle and needs to get to Zeths distance fast before it's too late.

"Don't wor worrrry ah about ma me, just ssaavve Zeth"

Clarified Cressida, in deep worry. With as much love and warmth as possible Lincent gently hugged Cressida as an assurance that will be aided in the final battle of the novel.

Meanwhile with Elargarious and Baxter.

Inside the office of Baxter Drastic, that looked like a cyberpunk vampires office, with cords connected all over the place, television screens showing more internet searches that had to be paid for, and many more electronics that hordes his room. Baxter was in his true form, looking like a rat with green eyes, he had a scar shaped like a goat emblem on left cheek, large rat tail with huge width, buff body, buff legs and wore a black suit and black pants. What Baxter was doing was raising his hand outside, and he spread his energy to influence the minds of the corrupt, and the weak for a desire to become transhumanist. Baxter was very successful in convincing them to transhumanism.

"As part of the deal, I shall offer you some of my gadgets for your god ascension, but in exchange for one thing which is to kill at least one 'righteously' per month, is that an agreement?" Stated Baxter whose energy was growing stronger on the minds of the people within City range.

"Agreed" Answered a thrilled Elargarious. Then a small amount of white energy was implementing second thoughts to a few individuals, that were being spiritually tempted by Baxter Drastic. "Look who it is, a Drastic traitor striving to be more like a righteousful, he's all yours Elargarious." Stated Baxter As Elargarious was running towards the hallway to reach to the door he saw dead security guards in many areas of the hallway. From a higher-level hallway, Zeth almost caught Elargarious by surprise while jumping onto him. But Elargarious grabbed a hold of Zeths body and was about to throw him onto the floor, until Zeth grabbed Elargarious's head and knee-kicked him on the beak.

Zeth has new clothes identical to the ones in chapter 1, which was from the vehicle that he was in. Elargarious made a small yell at what Zeth did, which caused him to let go. When Zeth got back on his feet he said, "Enough with the phoenix mask that hides your true self Jefferson and show me the real man who thinks he's the only one who exists." While holding his bloody beak, Elargarious smiled at Zeth and said.

"As a generous offer, I'll make it your dying wish." Clarified Elargarious who transformed into his cat-rat form, which was a much older looking Jefferson Drastic. Zeth looked at Jefferson with angry anxiety of excitement. Zeth was full-fledged spirited, by wanting to beat Jefferson up, and Jefferson knew that Zeth had a very serious attitude with him on this matter.

"You're going down" Exclaimed a vicious sounding and furious Zeth Drastic who is about to fight in the last chapter of 'Afternoon Solipsism'.

CHAPTER 9

Mizisipilop

STEALTHILY ZETH AND Jefferson advanced towards each other, in boxer stances. Jefferson preformed a left jab, but Zeth defended against the jab, and Jefferson reacted quickly to such attack by leaping away and leaping back towards Zeth. Jefferson preformed a boxing hook technique and Zeth dodged this move by crouching down. Zeth sent an uppercut, straight at Jefferson's right arm. That didn't stop Jefferson in the slightest, and he launched a more downwards overhand right cut to the top of Zeth's head. This hit Zeth's hat on impact and made Zeth determined to do a counter boxing technique that is called a 'cross-cut'. Zeth had to raise his arm and stand strategically for the process of doing this quick time event. The counter cross technique was unsuccessful because Jefferson managed to grab a hold of Zeths wrist by his left hand. The two then grabbed each other into a wrestling match. They both kicked at each other's legs, which caused both to fall and let go of each other. As Zeth and Jefferson were on the floor, they quickly got on their feet and were back in their boxing position again. Zeth's boxing stance was a 'semi-crouch', and Jefferson's stance, was an 'upright stance'. Zeth and Jefferson, walked around the hallway completely engaged and focused on each other. Zeth got close enough to punch Jefferson, and he used the left arm jab move unsuccessfully. However, Jefferson used the counter cross, which resulted to impact on Zeth's face. Jefferson's left overhand made impact on the right side of Zeth Drastics eye. Zeth changed his stance to a full crouch, and was taking a beating from Jefferson, who's attack potential was greater than the shattering of concrete. Zeth tried to do an uppercut with his left fist but Jefferson used a left jab so hard on Zeth's forehead that he couldn't finish the uppercut in time. Zeth went back to his semi-crouch stance and used the footwork defense to not get damaged by Jeffersons right jab. This gave Zeth the advantage to perform a leaping, right overhand, on Jeffersons mouth. Jefferson gave an angry look at what Zeth had done. He then delivered a left hook punch onto the upper right side of Zeth's head nearly hitting his temple. By using fast reaction speed, Zeth used a grappling position technique, which was on a stand position of the 'pinch grip tie.' For Zeth to do this he had to jump on Jefferson to accomplish such a technique.

The 'pinch grip tie' was close to being successful, but unfortunately for Zeth, Jeffersons legs and feet remained stationery during Zeth's attempted move. Jefferson advanced like a bull throwing Zeth into the air, landing him on the floor. However, Zeth is having trouble remaining still as he stands. In quick movement Jefferson chose a wrestling technique of his own liking. In truth, it was actually a professional technique called 'Chokeslam'. Jefferson applied the choke-slam by gripping each side of Zeth's Adams Apple, with a very tight squeeze. He lifts Zeth up and was about to slam his head on the floor, but Zeth punched the interior crook of Jefferson's elbow, causing two things to happen. 1. Jefferson's arm bent the way an arm is supposed to bend, and 2, this gave Zeth the advantage to do the 'Blockbuster". This caused Jefferson's head to crash through the concrete floor. Zeth kicked Jefferson for over a hundred meters away from him, and onto a steel pillar. As Jefferson fell down a hundred meters, he was almost completely out of energy. Zeth Drastic, was about to run to the staircase, until the gates to his destination closed in front of him. All the lights in the hallway were turned off. Only a red hologram of Baxter was seen on the center of the hallway. "I should have made a 'tisk tisk' over what you and Lincent did, and for kicking the bottom sacks of my somewhat organic, partially spirited piece of myself. You gave my uncle a bad night. Now!! what do you have to say for yourself?" Said Baxter who was speaking to Zeth. Zeth didn't answer Baxter. Zeth just gave a death threatening look at him, for what happened to Lincent. The ideal of him, even saying a word, is irrelevant! Zeth badly wanted to make Drofred/Baxter pay for what he did to Lincent.

"Well I guess your communication is offline with me now isn't it? No matter, I'll just speak to Uncle Jefferson." Said Baxter who turned to speak, directly to Jefferson.

If Zeth Drastic was greatly or vastly superior to Baxter? he would have made him miserable for a long time. The more Zeth viewed Baxters face, the more hatred built up inside of him. His desire is to make sure that Baxter would never hurt Lincent again.

"Do you want your power up uncle Jefferson?" Questioned Baxter.

Jefferson put forth effort in standing up after the critical blow that Zeth brought on him. Jefferson's face appeared bloody and bruised, from the crash landing on the steel pillar that was inside Baxter's building. and said in a psycho warden tone. "Yes"

After Jefferson spoke that word, Baxter clapped his hands, and Jefferson's body started to look like as if, giant beetles were invading his body. Zeth did not give an astonished stare during Jefferson's transformation. Grounded in a grudge to defeat Jefferson and Baxter, he was a little nervous as to what was going to happen next. Jefferson roared loudly, throughout the hallway! He was hurting bad from the procedures of his transhumanism.

"This is going to make my night! God, I love bot implants" Said Baxter, who turned to look at Zeth, for the sake of staring into the soul of his character. Jefferson's body was being stretched. His skin was torn from the process. New bones were becoming visible. These bones were gooey black and had slimy yellow and brown urine squirting out of it. Zeth and Baxter gave a 'cowboy western showdown' stare at each other. Baxter enjoyed the sight of Zeth's face of hatred.

"Have a good last time Zeth Drastic" After Baxter finished those words, the hologram turned off. Everything in the large hallway, was extremely difficult to see. Despite this fact, Zeth remained enraged during the heat of battle against Jefferson. However, something made Zeth feel a little more unnerved. It was the difficult sight of Jefferson's transformation.

The sounds of Jefferson yelling changed into electronic sounds, that also sounded like a kitten meowing in reverse. and then being shoved up their butt. More horrific sound effects were being heard in the distance ahead of Zeth. One, being that of a tongue lick on sand. Two a sexual intercourse sound effect. Three, someone opening and closing their butthole slowly with poop sounds that had no gas along with it. Four, teeth chattering at speeds racing faster than 1.15 times each second. Then, more teeth chattering sounds were being heard in a few seconds. Finally, Five, the crow and hyena sounds were being morphed together to make a maliciously evil laugh. Zeth did the best he could to hide, his fear from Jefferson's transformation. The tension grew immensely, and Zeth was nervous over Jefferson's new capabilities. Zeth, activated his gadgets, for defense, from Jefferson's new form, and advanced with caution. Using the gadgets made Zeth's muscles turn big and disruptive. He used 'the muscle ripper 1979, a strength that could lift and destroy buildings that were the size of the world trade center. Zeth wasn't sure about using 'the uber weighted ball', or the '75th Paward' yet, because these actions could go wrong. He was saving it as an element of surprise.

"Solly, sola salara solipsism, miss, missay, miss, mism, mismilop, misisipilop, miss, miss... Mizisipilop, me am the mizisipilop!" Exclaimed Jefferson whose voice kept cracking and squeaking, he is no longer known as Jefferson or Elargarious but as 'Mizisipilop'.

Suddenly, a flash back to the real world was set in motion. David powered back to his bright form, freed himself from Caprins powers and continued to fight. Caprin, fully manifested back into his real form, and did a blitz speed karate kick to David, but David hopped over Caprins foot, and karate kicked Caprin on the nose. Caprin, smacked David away with his wings that formed hurricanes far larger than Vy canis majoris. The hurricanes were going faster than the traveling speed, going over a heliocentric universe far less than a yoctosecond. However, those hurricanes didn't stop David, and he used his wings and flapped the giant hurricanes that were larger than vy canis majoris towards Caprin.

"These large star size twirls, are my storms now!" Said David who was about to unleash these hurricanes that were larger than vy canis majoris to his initiative. The size of the hurricanes grew larger than a heliocentric solar system. There were over a hundred trillion of them crashing into Caprin. This sent Caprin flying uncontrollably in every direction, which gave David the advantage to give a massive elbow slam on Caprins belly. David attempted to do this, by using the hurricanes guiding him. As an addition to the destructive force of the elbow slam, Caprin used 'Xifos Gia Midenismo' to defend himself., and used his upper left fist to punch Davids forehead. Caprin also attempted to chop David in half by using 'Xifos Gia Midenismo'. However, he did a magnificent U.C.S. kick on Caprins belly, that was far greater than a gamma ray burst and vy canis majoris supernova destructive capacity. With Caprin being away in a distance greater than a universe, David created a five-foot flaming katana far hotter than vy canis majoris and Eta Carinae times together. David did a Iaijutsu stance, and when Caprin got back in fighting position, he knew exactly what David was going to use, he could sense it. Caprin has the ability called 'We-mart-ense.' Certain specifics, possibly all martial arts, techniques that can be sensed by formation of combat with a near to masterful counteract or counterattack, this ability also grant's a power increase too.

Caprin, used 'Wemartense' very efficiently against Iaijutsu users. These were more than infinite times his duration, attack potency, speed, and strength. He counteracted and defeated them with ease.

As David preformed Iaijutsu, it led the distance speed that was far greater than a yoctosecond. Right before the very last yoctosecond within U.C.S, David changed this technique with an upward slice. The reason why he did this, is because of Caprins ability 'Welmartense' that would be a one shot at David. Caprin managed to dodge, while creating a steel plate which had the height higher than a galaxy, and width that was more than googleplexian times the size of a universe. Each cubit piece of it was more than googleplexian times, smaller than a proton, and weighs far much more than a universe.

The steel plate was glowing bright green and purple. This was the result of Caprin, using an ability called 'Crasength' which greatly increases the weight of something or someone far beyond its original weight. Caprin threw it towards David, who lifted it, spun around and threw it back at Caprin at a blitz speed. Caprin sliced the plate, that he could easily lift turning it into dust by using 'Xifos Gia Midenismo'. Caprin was growing tired of David equally combating him, in power. He counteracted with his abilities and decided to use an ability called 'Puzz-finisher'. This ability takes incomprehensible puzzle solving actions to complete. Failure to do so, will result in death. It should be noted, that this ability has killed many beings, that were above an infinite number of Infinites before. This power has managed to badly damage beings, that were above any infinity that science could comprehend. It reduces their duration, down to lower levels, that were in between human and universal. The appearance of the Ability was a blend of many colors and shapes. With multiple examples resembling Rubi cubes, changing colors, with a trillion shadowy octagons being squirted out of it. White soil formed into triangular shapes, which then turn into orange disks with flaming aura, circling around them.

Piñatas were morphing inside the white soil. This spawned out spikes of red grass shaped objects. The shadowy octagons began rubbing on the red grass shaped objects. This event caused, the explosion forming a skeletal image of a great Dane. The image flew around the explosion with an appearance of wine like mass as its wings.

Square shaped yellow serpents burst out of its neck and sung very off key, with random sounds coming out of their pupils. Tears from the serpents, erupted like a shaken soda being opened. The tears transformed into a power plant, that transformed into an actual plant, that is called a dandelion. These examples were only a very small representation of incomprehensible form. This form is 'Puzz-finisher'.

"Lame!" Said an insulting David. David knew he would have to act very soon. David used an ability called, 'Know-sive' which temporarily raises up someone's intelligence within the realm of nigh-omniscient and omniscient. With David's high intellect being active, he was able to comprehend the entire puzzle. David solved it within less than a yoctosecond. This action caused the puzzle, to show a long haired, long bearded, bright figure, torturing anthropomorphic people with a red devil toy. As the puzzle vanished, Caprin began to tap onto a power that was infinitely greater than duration. Gaining attack potency, speed, strength and possibly range. This power is called 'Dimenfoe first'. Another fun note is such a power from Dimenfoe, creating a hurricane larger than a universe, and they were both in it. The strange thing about this power is, when 'Xifos Gia Midenismo' is involved with it, the sword becomes infinitely greater than its lesser human to universal realm. 'Xifos Gia Midenismos' attack potency increases far much more than googleplexian times his cutting and slicing power and is more than googleplexian times the speed of its power. Endlessly increasing in the speed of one googleplexian of a yoctosecond. Dimenfoefirst also made Caprin appear very smoke like and was shown to be in a bit of static from time to time. David also used Dimenfoefirst and it made him comparable to Caprins Dimenfoe power.

From Caprins top right, he attempted to slice David in half going bottom left, however David dodged and punched the center of Caprins face.

"Fun feeling? am I right or are you just a step under?"

laughed an overconfident David.

Caprin used his left arm, and grabbed a hold of David, and began an attempt to try to crush him with his arms and wings. Caprin opened his mouth and was ready to chew off David's head.

Caprins mouth grew up to sixty inches in diameter. As David's head was almost within range of being eaten by Caprin, David did an arm wrestle tactic, where at first, he was casual in the match, but later gave one or two tilts and won.

David did a similar position by putting a little harder effort to the left and then fully spun around to the right. This caused him to spin around Caprins arms and wings and allowed him to slip upwards to the inside of Caprins mouth. This spinning movement looked like a tornado larger than a universe. This force of impact sent Caprin past the distance of a universe and faster than the speed of a yoctosecond within the infinite speed of Dimenfoe first. David's accomplishment, impressed Caprin so much that he used Dimenfoe second, which made him infinitely greater than Dimenfoe first.

"Going further than the higher destructive capacities, is so... something that's of ease to me." Said David. David quickly powered up to Dimenfoe second as well and flew after Caprin.

'Xifos Gia Midenismo" increased greater than its previous multiplication. Caprin was very close to cutting David into so many pieces beyond repair, but his appearance showed to be very static. Radio static sounds were heard coming from within him. Caprin's lack of ability to move, gave David the advantage to spin like a tornado and bring forth a massive right foot kick to Caprin's head.

David began to keep boxing Caprin's face until he was able to sledgehammer the top of Caprin's head until he appeared static. He couldn't move very well. Caprin was starting to move, and within the speed of Dimenfoe second, he slowly moved his right arm closer to David's shoulders.

As "Xifos Gia Midenismo" touched Davids shoulder, Caprin did the best he could, to saw David's left arm off. Caprin moved "Xifos Gia Midenismo" backwards, causing blood to squirt out from David, which made him squeal like a pig to the pain. Caprin moved "Xifo's Gia Midenismo" forwards. An extreme amount of blood was squirting out of David. Caprin was getting close to the bone part of David's shoulder. David reacted like someone being corrupted by a virus from a sci-fi horror film. Caprin moved Xifos Gia Midenismo backwards, while sawing over an inch of Davids bone.

When Caprin moved Xifos Gia Midenismo forward, Davids left arm was nearly all the way sawed off, and David yelled at such a high pitch that the sound waves were larger than a universe. The screech made Caprin cover his ears for a bit, and this gave David the opportunity to regenerate his arm, but Caprin got back in gear and used an ability called 'Shugen'. This ability can shut down a high level of regeneration and healing. It's possible to be at a nigh-omnipotent level. Strictly being capable of a healing factor and regeneration. Although it's limits are not fully known. This was an ability that Caprin regretted not using in chapter 7, against David's regeneration. Caprin chose to use a huge chunk of his power to make sure he didn't counteract 'Shugen' that easily.

So, David made a real gruesome effort in ripping off his left arm and creating life out of it. David did this, from learning how the Judgmisspast creates life. With the hand of the ripped arm that was popping out, David transformed the sword into a living organic sword, which had the appearance of skin being inside out. David channeled his energy to the sword, making it infinitely more powerful than before, with the power being called 'Dimenfoe third'. It multiplies the power of Dimenfoe second, by infinity, with duration, attack potency, speed, strength and possibly range being multiplied in the process.

Caprin managed to control Dimenfoe second, he used master cord block level 1 to combat against Davids swordsman attacks and boosted his sword with Dimenfoe third. Within Dimenfoe thirds speed of U.C.S, Caprin and Davids range of sword clashing was larger than a universe.

David was getting cut in a lot of areas on his hips, shoulders and legs by Caprin surpassing him in speed. Then David used his powers to transform his sword into a human shaped skin, turned inside out creature with golden angle wings and two whips on both its hands. The head turned into a red dragons face with black eyes and eight horns on the top of its skull. This creature stood over 12 feet high and fought Caprin with its four whips. While Caprin and the creature were fighting, this gave David the advantage in raising his hands into the sky for something very powerful. It was a bright light green orb of great power, it's level of multiplication is more than infinite of infinites and whoever eats this would temporarily possess its power. David managed to sink his teeth on half of it, and knew he had to act fast before it was too late. Caprin used a very tiresome and risky one-shot attack of Dimenfoe fifth, which made him infinitely more powerful than the four categories of duration, attack potency, speed, strength and possibly range. Dimenfoe fourth infinitely surpasses Dimenfoe third. Using Dimenfoe fifth gave Caprin one shot at the creature, and as he sunk his teeth on the orb, in front of David, both halves of the orb went into their throats, a burst of flames and dark clouds that were far larger than a universe was combating against each other physically and spiritually. They were also trying to channel the energy of the minds of the people with images of a bearded old man with white robes turning children into elderly people dying, while yelling in pain. It shows a white rabbit healing them with yellow energy and turning them back into youth.

** It should be noted that Eogo possesses what Caprin and David can do in chapter 7-9 and is vastly superior to them. Even if Caprin and David teamed up together in a 'mlvfg' against Eogo Ali Tainter, they would most surely lose.

The collision of impact from Caprin and David, was so strong, that the power of the orb faded away. They were both knocked out unconscious and were blasted all the way down to the hills at 3:20 AM.

Meanwhile with Lincent

Lincent rode on a black motorcycle, to reach to her destination. She now had to analyze and pay attention to her surroundings. She wasn't fully sure how Baxter established, his creations. Lincent wasn't completely helpless in figuring things out, on how their made. Lincent just doesn't know everything about it. What Lincent does know is a transhumanist Drofreds duration and attack potency, ranges from a small town to a city. Second, their speed is estimated to be what it's stated in chapter 3 of Afternoon Solipsism. Thirdly, the Drofred that Lincent was facing in chapter 3, wasn't really Baxter but one of his more least favorite creations. He had to make it because he lost a bet with Carl, and the failure was to make him create a humiliating creation of his younger self. It had less of a serious attitude, than what he has now. **For example, when Lincent kicked the bottom of Drofreds testicles, he asked for his mother to help him, but if Lincent hit the bottom of Baxters testicles, he would either give an angry look at Lincent or take it like a man and continue fighting.

Baxter isn't like who he was before and doesn't have childlike behaviors when losing anymore. Baxter sometimes makes mistakes. He has improved drastically and is progressing further. Baxter has questioned his motives, by using transhumanism for god ascension like Jerico, not in the sense of 'I feel the struggle of good in me' but more towards the question of 'is defeating the all-powerful creator necessary for improving humanity? Or would Baxter be better off without the motives of the Insintation, and help the Rightiousful, by using his creations to improve for the better, while serving under the creator of everything?

This was a topic Lincent was interested in., She needed to stay on topic with the other things she knew about. Example, transhumanist Drofred which is number four. After all that, Lincent and her friends could gather from a transhumanist Drofreds abilities in them. They would be able to stun, analyze, steal memories and turn invisible.

Number five is about the transhumanist Drofred's weaknesses. Lincent has found out nothing on the problems or flaws of the transhumanist Drofreds. There is only one thing that Lincent is aware of, and that's, them having a crucial weakness. This is all about the possibility of a transhumanist Drofred losing control of the energy that is contained within them. The contained energy is in their robotic bellies or backs. How it is made, is Baxter placing spiritual energy into the trans-humanist Drofreds.

Baxter usually uses his own power, onto the transhumanist Drofreds.

He never uses or takes power from others. Carl on the other hand sure does. like stealing energy for his or her machines. Baxter feels more comfortable with his own energy being used in the transhumanist Drofreds and not much from anyone else.

The weaknesses were:

If a transhumanist Drofred overloads the energy that it contains within itself, it could self-destruct and blow up an entire city.

If a transhumanist Drofred's contained energy is tampered with, it could either… A. go haywire with initiatives and consistency on motives/goals or, B. result in the same effect of what the previous sentence has clarified.

The question for Lincent using this weakness, is how is she going to set the time limit for the explosion to be explosion active, and how is she going to get the civilians out of danger from the explosion? Lincent could only think of one solution of getting the civilians out of danger and setting the time limit for the transhumanist Drofreds. It was to use one of the trans-humanists Drofreds voice on the intercom to warn the people of the explosion that is to come.

As Lincent arrived at her destination she could see blood on the glass panels of the doors to the hallway that Zeth entered in. Lincent was scared for Zeth's safety, knowing that there was a possibility of him getting killed, by Drofred or Elargarious. Lincent wanted to make sure Zeth was all right but knew that if she didn't put a stop to Drofred's transhumanist agenda, that he could lead people astray. Stopping their belief, and their serving under an all-powerful creator. Lincent's feelings for Zeth might not even be just her caring for him, but something much more. Lincent wasn't sure about, how to express these true feelings that she felt for Zeth yet. She feels as if she needs to eventually let him know the truth about what their relationship can be and possibly will be.

The temptation to rush in there and save Zeth was strong, but if Lincent did, she'd blow her element of surprise and Drofred would come prepared, for what she would try to do.

Suddenly! Lincent heard painful screams, that sounded like Zeth.

This caused Lincent to temporarily lose, her planned mindset, and her goals. She almost chose to fully run in and save Zeth. Lincent stopped and maintained self-control, and returned to what she needed to be consistent, in doing. Quickly Lincent looked around for a way into the building. She saw one of the guards go into an entrance, that few of the guards had been using. With the entrance being the lesser entered one, Lincent decided to use it.

The door of the entrance looked like any black door, with the difference being that it required a small blood sample from the swat members to gain access, while being stationed in the off-limits areas of Drofred's headquarters. Lincent saw an opportunity, eyeing a swat member walking to the direction of the door. This gave Lincent the advantage to go silently and leapj behind the guard and knock him out.

Meanwhile with Baxter.

In Baxter's office, Baxter was watching a security camera that showed the fight between Zeth and Mizisipilop. Sounds from the video camera were screams of Zeth getting badly beaten. Baxter was a little pleased with the results of Jeffersons, however Baxter was not as pleased as Carl would be in this situation. Baxter wasn't like Carl, who does whatever he or she can do, in gaining pleasure from some one's sorrow.

The reason why Baxter was happy, with Zeth being beaten, was Zeth kept trying to bring the Insintation down. Baxter gained so many resources, from what the Insintation granted him, because of Zeth trying to foil the Insintation, it would come at a cost of Baxter losing a lot of his resources. With Zeth accomplishing such a goal, destroying the Insintation, would be extremely difficult to get done. Most who work for the Insintation believe Zeth will fail miserably, in defeating Insintation. The one who is second to command, 'Caprin the bat' believes that it is possible for Zeth to overcome his struggles in defeating the Insintation and putting an end to Eogos death comings of 'the doom without blood' before it's too late.

Baxter remembered what Crig's crown-pillar dark IX was being built up to be and feared it. Baxter loved the fact that the Insintation gave him the supplies and resources for the makings of his transhumanist creations and loved how Jerico made a great deal of influence on him in doing so. Crig's crown was a nightmare fuel, even argued to be the nightmare fuel incarnate. Crig's crown has been known to possess ridiculous horror ambiguity of every character losing complete sight of who they are. Crig's crown sets the course of making a character unglued and unresolved. The more Baxter thinks about Crig's crown, the more he wants to abandon the Insination, and help the ones who are opposed to them. Or maybe Baxter could improve on his transhumanist invention, so well that he could destroy Crigs crown, and guide the world in his image. This is not going to happen, this is stated by Eogo, that no man born of sin or from sin can destroy Crigs crown. Baxter wants to deny Eogos claim on this, but no Insination questions Eogo Ali Tainter ever. Baxter didn't want to think of failing his prevention of Crigs Crown. He now, only wanted to see Zeth get punishment for his actions. Suddenly the intercom was heard, with a voice that sounded exactly like his.

"In less than ten minutes, a bomb will blast within city range. leave now!!! Before it's too late!" this message repeated every 30 seconds.

This caused a difficulty for Baxter, not to panic on the outside, and try his hardest to contain it on the inside. Baxter was in disbelief on such destructive potential and knew he had to get out of the bombs explosions within city range. There was no way he could undo such imbalance, in energy containment.

Meanwhile with Zeth

Zeth had a lot of trouble seeing Mizisipilop, and he tried his best not to overuse the muscle ripper and Paward. Instead he chose to use the gadgets to the highest level. Mizisipilop was getting stronger faster, and gained more duration increase, by taking hits from Zeth, and using the muscle ripper and Paward at full power.

Zeth could not depend on his eyes, in this situation. Zeth needed to use his ears and feelings. focusing on the floor, indicating where Mizisipilop footsteps were coming from. The footsteps were vague. Due to how fast Mizisipilop has become, Zeths full power in speed with Paward in comparison to Mizisipilops, was now like comparing an average human to a cheetah. This would imply that Mizisipilop has been moving all around Zeth, as an attempt to attack him on a least defensive target. This caused Zeth to sweat a bit and breathe a little slower at the tension of Mizisipilop trying to claw him into pieces. Then Zeth had an idea that he did not feel comfortable in using, because it was something he viewed as a cruel mind rape tactic for survival. It worked the last time when Mizisipilop was attacking Jefferson. How would it be put into effect now? in the abominable transhumanism he has undergone both. It was difficult to tell, but this might be Zeth's only option to beat Mizisipilop.

The laughs were being heard all around Zeth, and he knew that this blast energy on Mizisipilops mind will need to be right on him to make the mind rape more effective. Zeth continued to gather a conjured up spiritual energy, feeling alone, that all is fake, that Jefferson only had himself and the rest never really existed. Zeth could feel the kind of sorrow Jefferson felt with this feeling of being alone as a matter of fact Zeth didn't even like channeling this type of energy. It just didn't feel good at all, a Rightiousful does not like using mind rape alternatives.

The footsteps were vague, and due to how fast Mizisipilop has become, Zeths full power in speed with Paward in comparison to Mizisipilops, was now like comparing an average human to a cheetah, which implies that Mizisipilop has been moving all around Zeth as an attempt to attack him on a least defensive target. This caused Zeth to sweat a bit and breathe a little slower at the tension of Mizisipilop trying to claw him into pieces. Then Zeth had an idea that he did not feel comfortable using, because it was something he viewed as a cruel mind rape tactic for survival. It worked the last time, when Mizisipilop was Jefferson, but how would it be put into effect now in the abominable transhumanism he has undergone, of both and mind. It's difficult to tell, but this might be Zeth's only option to beat Mizisipilop.

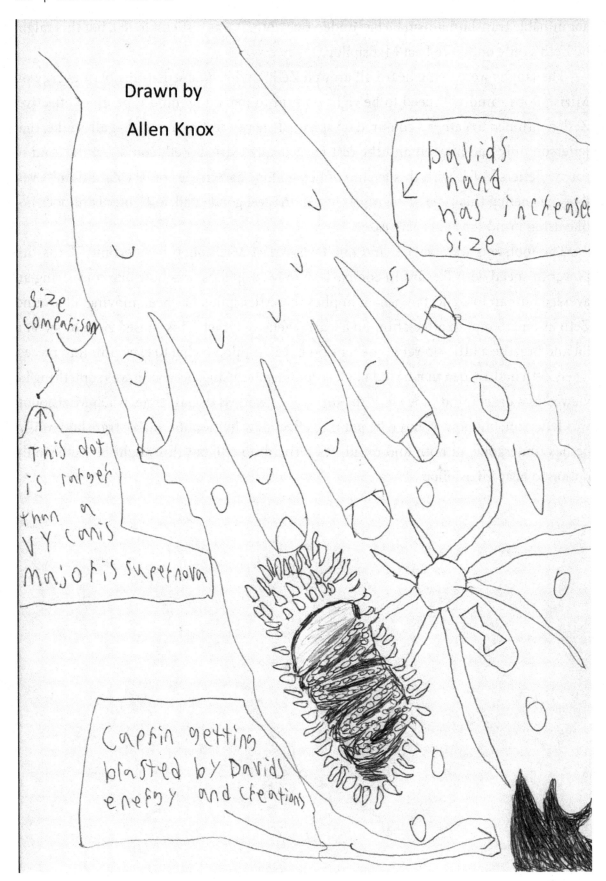

The laughs were being heard all around Zeth, and he knew that this blast of energy on Mizisipilops mind will need to be right on him to make the mind rape more effective. Zeth continued to gather a conjured up spiritual energy of feeling alone, that all is fake, that Jefferson only had himself and the rest never really existed. The footsteps were combat quiet. Due to how fast Mizisipilop had become, Zeths full power in speed with Paward in comparison to Mizisipilops, was now like comparing an average human to a cheetah. This implies that Mizisipilop has been moving stealthily around Zeth, as an attempt to attack him on a least defensive operation of attack. This caused Zeth to sweat a bit and breathe a little slower at the tension of Mizisipilop trying to claw him into pieces. Out of nowhere Zeth had an idea, that he did not feel comfortable in using, because it was something he viewed as a cruel mind rape tactic for survival. This attack worked the last time, when Mizisipilop was Jefferson, but how would it be put into effect now? With the abominable transhumanism he had undergone, from both and mind.

It's difficult to tell, but this might be Zeth's only option to beat Mizisipilop. The laughs were being heard all around Zeth, and he knew that this blast energy on Mizisipilops mind will need to be directly targeted on him to make the mind rape more effective. Zeth continued. He gathered a conjured up spiritual energy of feeling alone, that all is fake. Jefferson only had himself and the rest never really existed. Zeth could feel the kind of sorrow Jefferson felt, with this feeling of being alone, as a matter of fact Zeth didn't even like channeling this type of energy. It just didn't feel good at all, a Rightiousful does not like using mind rape alternatives because of the effects of the ability.

The Zeth Drastic of this timeline is not fond of sadism, however if getting the jobs are limited, using sadistic abilities would become the only way to beat the enemy. He'll likely use it. From the left side of Zeths shoulder Mizisipilop tried to slice Zeth in half and Zeth dodged though the hearing and feelings of the footsteps. Now the spiritual mind rape energy has been full and Zeth was ready to use it. Listening, and feeling, the steps carefully, Zeth noticed that something was off patern, with Mizisipilops footsteps. The 'speed movement', goes from extremely fast, to slow, randomly. When Zeth thought, Mizisipilop at a certain area, the sounds seemed to come from a different direction. Zeth had to react fast, and counter act, Mizisipilops next attack. Zeth chose to use Paward, and muscle ripper, as an addition to impact on Mizisipilop. Zeth did a fake reaction, by paying attention to where the sounds and footsteps of Mizisipilop were making impact. Zeth made it seem, as if, he was going to attack from in front of him. He quickly turns around and with the spiritual energy, speed, and strength, of Paward and Muscle ripper, Zeth punched Mizisipilop right on the forehead.

The energy of impact temporarily showed, what Mizisipilop looked like, with eagle heads, Jabbing around Jefferson's neck. Jefferson's head and neck, were blood red. His eyes were that of a chimpanzee, his legs with torn bloody skin, that showed it had been stretched to a tall length. The chest and belly were green with yellow puss squirting out of it. The arms were nothing, but bone scattered in length, longer than his body. The hands were covered in blood being large, and the fingers appearing as if they were talons.

All around Jefferson, was blood from the beaks, that were jabbed onto his neck. The impact of Zeth's punch, that could have destroyed the world trade center, caused a small crack on Jefferson's forehead.

This angered Mizisipilop and with a destructive force, similar to Zeth's punch, kicked Zeth away from him. Mizisipilop panicked with zero self-control and started to try and kill himself with the sharp beaks sticking in him. Zeth gave it his all. He stood up and ran after Mizisipilop. Advancing, he went behind Mizisipilop and strangled him. He used the weighted ball, being activated while using muscle ripper as a boost of strength to strangle This Mizisipilop any further.

Drawn by
Allen KNox

This brutal strangulation gave Zeth the opportunity he needed to tie the chains around Mizisipilops throat, and leave with the weighted ball, keeping Mizisipilop down. Zeth ran as fast as he could to the exit door. Thanks to Baxter it was locked, and Zeth did everything he could to open the door. Nothing worked, until he used the muscle ripper. He punched the door open and got out of Drofreds headquarters. After that fiasco, Zeth got back into the truck, and rode out of there.

Meanwhile with Mizisipilop

Mizisipilop was getting larger. Mizisipilop could survive a city destructive range level, with his potential. Unfortunately for Mizisipilop, he couldn't escape in time, to avoid the explosion. Now he must withstand the explosion that will do great damage to him. The explosion had an impact on the whole city range. Caprin flew down towards the aftermath of it, he saw Jeffersons flesh melted, destroyed body of bones was completely gone. The current time of explosion was 5:25 AM, and the melted Mizisipilop who was, Jefferson, gasped for air to breath in a nasty manner. Caprin mercy kills Jefferson by grabbing his head and squeezed it like a teenage pimple.

Meanwhile with Zeth and Lincent

Zeth made it back to the house where Lincent was being treated, he saw Lincent getting off the motorcycle running up to him. Without thinking, Zeth immediately stopped the vehicle, and got out. He ran up and hugged Lincent, with a comfort, exhausted with what they both had been through. It was indeed a tough night, but Lincent was so glad to know that Zeth was ok. Zeth couldn't have been more grateful, that Lincent was alive and well, and to be there for him no matter, the struggle. The energy between, emerged from pressing onto each other. It was like the fulfillment of going through a snow storm and at the end of it, having a nice warm bath.

Lincent was so pleased of Zeth being with her, that she was beginning to tremble and Zeth could physically feel it. Because of this, Zeth did the opposite of what he did to Mizisipilop and used his spiritual energy on Lincent to help ease her mind from the night they were in.

Lincent wasn't alarmed or defensive at Zeths efforts. His mind comfort on her, enforced a feeling of appreciation for Zeth, and she began to cry happily on his chest. Zeth eyes were tired from the previous fights he'd been through, but during his hard times, he arrived with a slight grin on his face. Knowing that this love Zeth has built on, with the relationship of the friends he'd been around for years made him have a sense of hope, that pain will be no more. That he may be away from the evil that is nothing for the good of everything, that makes you something.

There were so many questions to ask of the events happening in 'Afternoon Solipsism', such as was Nortric speaking to Sam in chapter 3 even real? Eogos past, Crigs crown, Zeths relationship with Nortric.

There's so much going on with Zeth and Lincent's mind, about what has happened this night. However, they need a good day's rest for the next steps that are to come.

Meanwhile in the sky at 5:35 AM

So high up in the darkness of the sky where the sun cannot shine, where nothing is seen, that is never seen showed. The anthropomorphic bat who was more than double Zeths age and flew many universal light speeds from beginning to end, with no effort. This force of impact would have shattered a steel box larger than vy canis majoris. This novel has come to an end, so the bat flew towards the moon for the doom without bloom.

THE END

THE END

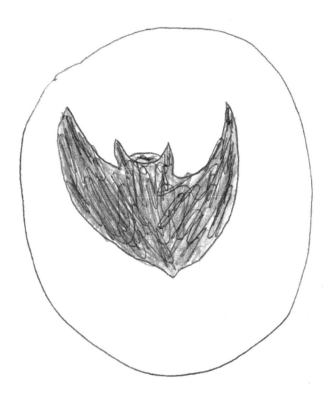

OR IS THIS, JUST THE BEGINNING?

Drawn by

Allen Knox

THE END

Printed in the United States
By Bookmasters